John's Cravings

John's Cravings

Nathan Jay

JNJ Publishing LLC

CONTENTS

CONTENTS

CONTENTS

For my grandmother, Mrs. Pearlene Jones

1

The Field Trip

"Where's Terrell?" asked Mrs. Bloom.

The teacher quickly searched up and down her line of students waiting to get on the school bus. After failing to find the child, Mrs. Bloom called out to Terrell's usual partner in mischief, Christopher.

"Christopher, have you seen Terrell?"

The child responded the way he usually did—he stared at the teacher with a surprised look and shrugged.

"No, ma'am, I haven't."

Mrs. Bloom didn't have time to play interrogator with Christopher. Panic was setting in, and the other teachers might notice her incompetence. She was the primary teacher responsible for the children on field trips, and she'd only been at the school for a few months. How would it look to the others if she lost one of the students?

Mrs. Bloom went back inside the museum to the gift counter, where a short, chubby lady was arranging rows of toy dinosaurs.

"Excuse me, we're missing one of our students. Have you seen a . . . ?"

The woman pointed toward the dinosaur exhibit before Mrs. Bloom could finish her sentence.

"There. I saw a little boy over there."

Mrs. Bloom walked quickly to the towering set of bones and looked around. The few lights shining on the gigantic dinosaur bones made the corners of the room dark. Mrs. Bloom sighed in frustration. The museum was the perfect place for a naughty child to escape detection. And because Terrell was more troublesome than most, Mrs. Bloom would have to manually check each corner of the enormous room in search of the boy.

"Terrell Mayfield!" Mrs. Bloom yelled while walking to the first corner. "If you're in here, you'd better come out! Everyone's getting on the bus!"

There was nothing in the first corner, so Mrs. Bloom walked quickly around the triceratops exhibit to the next dark corner.

Once again, the corner was empty. Mrs. Bloom was scared now. Losing a kid was a big deal, and the parents would be furious. When all was said and done, she'd probably lose her job.

Mrs. Bloom sighed in defeat, dug in her purse, and pulled out her cell phone to call the other teachers for help. As soon as she started dialing, she spotted movement in the corner behind the giant T-Rex.

"Terrell!" she snapped while rushing to the spot. "You can bet we'll have a conversation about following instructions."

When Mrs. Bloom arrived at the corner, she dropped her cell phone and screamed. Terrell was lying on the floor naked and covered in mud. The child's body was twitching and jerking as though something invisible was moving him. The convulsions lifted his tiny frame a few feet into the air before slamming him violently onto the concrete floor. Three long black blisters ran across Terrell's torso as though someone had branded him with a hot poker. Terrell's eyes were open, but he was unconscious, blood pouring from the corners of his mouth.

"Dear God! Terrell!" yelled Mrs. Bloom as she rushed to him. She tried grabbing the convulsing child's legs, but he was too powerful— Terrell's tiny leg kicked her in the chest and sent her sliding across the floor.

Determined to calm her student, Mrs. Bloom rose to her feet and jumped on top of the boy. Suddenly, an odor entered Mrs. Bloom's nostrils so powerful that she became nauseous. The thick substance covering the child's body wasn't mud—it was human feces. The stench was so unbearable that Mrs. Bloom couldn't control herself; she turned her head and vomited all over the floor.

Mrs. Bloom finished throwing up and wiped the vomit from her chin. She removed her scarf from her neck and wiped chunks of the human waste from the boy's face.

"Terrell. Oh my God, what happened?" she asked the child.

Suddenly Terrell's eyes began blinking. After looking all around the room, his eyes fell on his teacher.

"Please, Mrs. Bloom, get me out of here. He's coming for me."

Mrs. Bloom wiped Terrell's face and held him close.

"Who's coming for you? Who did this to you?"

Once again, Terrell's eyes rolled in his head, and he jerked violently, sending his teacher sailing again through the air.

But this time, Mrs. Bloom prepared for her landing and quickly kicked her feet against the wall before she could smash into it. She flipped onto her belly, jumped to her feet, and started yelling for help.

"Someone, please! Come quick!"

Within seconds, the chubby woman at the gift counter appeared. She looked at the child having convulsions on the ground, and froze.

"Oh my God!" the woman screamed.

Mrs. Bloom didn't have a lot of time. The blood pouring from Terrell's mouth seemed to be getting worse.

"Get security!"

"But I don't understand. What happened?"

"Goddamnit, get help! Now!"

Finally, the woman took off running through the museum.

"Don't worry, Terrell. Everything's going to be okay."

At that moment, Mrs. Bloom remembered her cell phone. She'd dropped it on the floor when she screamed. Frantically, she searched in the dark until she found the phone beside Terrell in a pool of excrement. Mrs. Bloom grabbed the device, wiped it off, and dialed 911.

Before someone answered, the lights in the museum turned on, and the security guards rushed into the room.

Not the Same

Penny sipped her glass of wine and stared across the dining room table at her son, Terrell. The boy sat silently at the table, staring down at the plate.

"Terrell, the steak's delicious. Won't you take a bite?" Penny asked.

Terrell didn't move.

Penny sighed. It had been three weeks since the incident at the museum, and Terrell wasn't getting any better; the boy wasn't saying more than two words, and his malaise seemed to worsen daily. He'd stopped eating and drinking and no longer went outside to play with the other children. Instead, Terrell sat on the sofa or in his bedroom, staring into nothingness. Terrell had even stopped going to the bathroom, urinating right where he sat or laid. Penny was furious the first time Terrell peed while standing in the living room. But as soon as she tried disciplining the child, her heart sank—Terrell wasn't there and didn't seem to know what he'd done.

So, Penny adjusted. She started walking Terrell to the bathroom and waiting until he finished. Penny avoided the living room and sat him in a chair on the linoleum floor. She woke up twice for bathroom breaks during the night to ensure he didn't wet the bed; there was a strange odor in Terrell's bedroom, and Penny wanted to ensure it didn't get out of hand. Still, Terrell seemed to pull away even further emotionally.

Sometimes, she'd see Terrell lying in bed with his eyes open, staring into the darkness when she checked on him.

Penny and her husband strategized the best way to deal with their son, but they didn't have a solution to raise him from his emotional descent. The Terrell they knew, who was usually so vibrant and filled with life, was gone. Instead, what returned from the museum was an empty shell of a child that neither Penny nor Donavan recognized.

And then there were Terrell's injuries.

Although the doctors told her that Terrell had only suffered minor burns and would recover fully, the three large black blisters across his torso scared Penny. One morning, after she put medicine on Terrell's burns, the burns seemed to get better. But the following day, when Penny removed Terrell's shirt for inspection, the burns were different and seemed to grow, becoming puffier and spreading across Terrell's chest like a fluid-filled blanket. Remembering how her mother had treated a burn she suffered as a child, Penny retrieved a hat pin and decided to pop the blisters while Terrell slept. As soon as she pierced the blister, a vile smell filled the room, causing her to gag. Holding her breath, Penny quickly grabbed a towel and tried squeezing the fluid out of the wound. But instead of clear liquid, a thick tar-like substance poured out, staining the bed and floor.

Penny immediately took her son to the hospital. After running some tests, the doctors told her once more that the burns were typical and posed no threat. The fluid, the doctors said, was Terrell's body healing itself, and the smell was a slight infection curable with antibiotics. Feeling angry and afraid, with the stench of the black goo heavy in her nose and mouth, Penny took her son home, placed him in the guest room, and disinfected the whole house.

Penny struggled to understand what had happened on that field trip. When she met the school principal, the man gave her a lame excuse, half blaming Terrell for wandering away while also blaming the museum for the poor lighting, carefully sidestepping ownership of the school's inadequate supervision. Furious with the principal's attempt at evading responsibility, Penny went home and called her attorney that same day. But now Penny was here with what was left of her son, trying to understand what happened to him.

Penny tried once more to communicate with her son.

"What's wrong, Terrell?" she asked.

The child's face remained stoic as he stared at the piece of steak on his plate. Unsure of what to say, Penny shot a worried expression at her husband while Donavan motioned for her to be patient.

"Isn't steak your favorite, Terrell?" asked Donavan.

Terrell didn't budge.

"You need help cutting the steak? Here, let me help you."

Donavan raised himself from the table and moved behind Terrell. As soon as he reached out for the boy's knife and fork, Terrell recoiled and knocked over the glass of water, sending his plate of food sprawling.

"He's coming! I see him!" yelled Terrell.

The child rolled out of the chair and curled himself into a ball underneath the table.

"Terrell," whispered Donavan. "It's me, Daddy."

"No . . . No . . . No . . ." Terrell repeatedly whispered, trembling while cupping his palms over his ears.

Donavan stood frozen in surprise as he watched his son shaking on the floor.

Penny got up from the table, ran to Terrell's side, and rubbed his back gently.

"Don't worry, baby. Mommy's here. Everything's okay."

Donavan looked on nervously.

"I don't know what happened. He's never reacted like that before. As soon as I grabbed the knife and fork, he . . ."

But Penny didn't hear Donavan because she was too terrified to listen. Terrell was sweating so much that his shirt was wet. She could feel his heart racing, and his breathing was labored.

"Call Dr. Williams."

"It's too late, and they'll only tell us to go to the emergency room. Besides, Dr. Williams said this would happen for a while until his mind let go of the—"

"Well, do something other than just standing there!"

Donavan lifted Terrell from the ground.

"Come on, little guy. Let's move you to the bedroom."

Donavan carried his son upstairs with a worried Penny following closely behind.

"Don't worry, baby," said Penny. "Mommy and Daddy will take care of you."

After arriving at the bedroom, Donavan kicked open the door. A pungent odor flooded out into the hall as soon as he did.

"Jesus! Why does his room smell? Did he take a shit in here or something?" complained Donavan.

Penny covered her nose.

"Gosh! I disinfected his room with bleach, but the smell was still there. I'll have to pull his mattress out of here in the morning."

"Turn on the lights."

Penny fumbled along the wall until she found the light switch. She flipped it, and nothing happened.

"It's not turning on."

"Goddamnit."

Donavan laid Terrell on the bed and tried turning on the lamp next to the bed. Nothing happened.

"That's strange. The other lights in the house are working fine except for here. We must've blown a fuse or something. I'll go downstairs to check it out."

Penny sat on the bed beside Terrell while Donavan ran down the stairs. Penny couldn't see her son's face in the darkness, but she kissed his cheek and ran her fingers through his hair.

"Everything's going to be okay, baby. Mommy's here."

After a while, the lights in the bedroom flashed on and then off again.

"Did that get it?" yelled Donavan from downstairs.

"The lights came on but went out again!" yelled Penny.

"Damn it! Hold on!" replied Donavan.

Penny listened while Donavan fumbled around downstairs. Finally, the lights came on and stayed.

"Okay! They're on!" she yelled.

"What? I can't hear you!" replied Donavan.

Penny walked to the door and yelled.

"I said it's on!"

Donavan came sprinting up the stairs and stopped at the door.

"Where's Terrell? The bathroom?"

Penny spun around and looked at the bed. Terrell was gone.

"What? He was just . . ."

Penny ran to the bed and looked behind it, but he wasn't there. She fell to her knees and lifted the blanket to look underneath the bed—Terrell wasn't there, either.

Donavan walked to the child's bathroom and flipped on the light.

"He's not in here. What the fuck?"

Suddenly, a terrifying thought came into Penny's mind, and her eyes met Donavan's.

"No. He couldn't have . . ."

Donavan ran to the window and looked down on the lawn. After seeing nothing but the security lights shining on the empty yard, he sighed and turned back to talk to his wife.

"He's not out there. Good, at least he didn't jump. But still, I don't get it. Where did he go?"

But Penny didn't hear him. By the time Donavan turned around, she was downstairs searching the house.

"Terrell!" she screamed as she searched the living room and the kitchen. "Baby, where are you?"

Soon Penny's eyes fell on the door leading to the basement, and she had another frightening thought. What if Terrell had fallen down the basement stairs? She remembered how afraid he was of the dark. The idea of him tumbling down the stairs and lying helpless in the darkness was too much for Penny. Slowly, she grabbed the doorknob and opened it.

"Terrell? Are you down there?" she called out from the stairs.

Penny listened, waiting for a response but heard nothing. She was about to close the basement door and head outside to continue her search when she heard a loud thump.

"Terrell! Is that you?"

The muffled sound of a child gagging followed another thunderous pounding that shook the floor.

"Terrell! Don't worry. Mommy's coming."

Penny felt for the light switch and turned it on. As soon as she did, she saw Terrell lying on the ground at the bottom of the stairs. He was naked, curled up in a ball, sweating profusely.

"Oh my God! Terrell!" yelled Penny. She was about to run down the stairs when Donavan grabbed her arm.

"Wait," Donavan said as he looked at the boy.

Penny was beside herself.

"Wait?! You wait! That's my son down there!"

Penny attempted to jerk her arm away from Donavan's, but he held firm and forcefully pulled his wife away from the stairs.

"That's not our son," he whispered without taking his eyes off the child.

The child began trembling and made several more gagging sounds before rolling onto his stomach.

Penny looked again at the child. Donavan was right. The child lying at the bottom of the stairs wasn't their son. Penny didn't understand why she hadn't noticed it before, but the child didn't look like Terrell. The boy was grotesquely thin; the ribs of his tiny body moved up and down with every breath he took. At the base of the child's skull was a long, thick vein stretched out into smaller veins throughout the boy's back.

"What the hell is going on?" asked Penny.

"Close the door. We'll call the police," replied Donavan.

As soon as Penny reached out to close the door, the child thrashed back and forth violently on the floor.

"Oh my God! We've got to help him!" yelled Penny.

Donovan pushed his wife aside and slammed the door closed.

"Call the police! Now!"

"But . . ."

"Goddamn it, Penny! Just call the fucking cops!"

Suddenly the couple heard another thunderous crash accompanied by a child screaming. Penny looked at Donavan, whose face was white as a bedsheet.

"We've got to go down there."

"Penny . . . call the cops, okay?"

Penny ran over to the telephone and picked it up. She began dialing, but her fingers felt as fat as sausages, and Penny misdialed. Suddenly the lights went out. Terrified, Penny moved her face close to the phone and tried dialing from memory. Then the tones of her dialing stopped.

"Donavan!" she whispered while pressing numbers randomly. "The phone died."

Penny hung up the phone and turned around to face her husband.

"What are we going to do?"

Donavan took one step toward Penny, and the basement door exploded, sending him sliding across the kitchen floor until he laid moaning at Penny's feet.

"Donavan!" Penny screamed.

She grabbed her husband by the arm and tried to lift him off the floor.

"Aaaahh!" he screamed.

"Donavan! What is it?" Penny replied.

"My . . . back," Donavan groaned.

Penny inspected her husband and saw a large piece of wood stuck in his shoulder.

"Oh my God!" she screamed.

Penny was about to extend her arm to help Donavan to his feet but froze. Something wasn't right.

"What's happening? I can't move!" she screamed.

Donavan tried to get up to help Penny.

"Oh my God! I can't move, either!"

Penny tried again to reach out to her husband, but she could not move her hands and legs. Tears began pouring down her face as she stared at Donavan—his face white with fear, struggling through his injury and bleeding, powerless to stop it.

Soon a familiar odor filled the room, causing Penny to gag. It was the same odor she smelled in her son's bedroom, except it was more intense and distinct this time: human feces, rotten eggs, and maple syrup. The combination of odors made Penny's stomach churn, and her lips quivered. But something else bothered Penny about the smell—there was a familiarity to it that only she could discern. Soon Penny discovered why the smell repulsed her.

"Beaver Lake," she whispered.

Beaver Lake was where she almost drowned when she was a child. The recollection overpowered Penny, and she screamed. It all came rushing back to her like a nightmare. She could feel everything about that day: the freezing water, the terrified look on her father's face as he looked down into the water, the fingertips of death tugging at Penny's lungs, trying to get her to take a breath.

"Babe! Can you move?" asked Donavan struggling to free himself. "Snap out of it!"

But Penny couldn't hear him. The odor took over her senses and turned her digestive system against her. Loud gurgling sounds pushed forth from her throat, and she began drooling a foamy white mess from her mouth. A thick line of snot dripped slightly from one nostril and started pouring out of both nostrils within seconds, running down her chin onto the floor.

"Penny!"

"Help . . . help me, Donavan."

Next, loud grumbling noises came from Penny's stomach, and her eyes widened in surprise. Both Donavan and Penny stared at her stomach, watching it move violently back and forth.

"Something's inside," exclaimed Donavan.

"Ahhhhh! It hurts!" Penny screamed, unable to double over. The long deep growl came from Penny's stomach again, and she closed her eyes.

"No," she whispered.

Suddenly Penny's shirt flew open, exposing her breasts and stomach.

"Donavan!" she screamed.

Penny's chest felt strange and warm inside, like she'd drank a cup of hot coffee. She started sweating and breathing heavily, unable to catch her breath. The warm feeling in her chest was now painful; it radiated from her waist to her clavicles.

"It hurts!" she screamed. "Help me, Donavan!"

Suddenly Penny's bra burst into flame.

"AAAHHHH!"

Penny thrashed back and forth as the fire engulfed her face, charring her neck and chin before igniting her hair. Within seconds her hair was gone, her face a burned mess.

And then, suddenly, the fire was gone.

Penny could move again. Her hands immediately flew to her neck and head—her hair was still there. She looked down.

"Oh my God! Donavan!"

Penny was terrified to see a large black blister covering her breasts and stomach.

"Donovan! Help me, please!"

"Penny! Baby! We've got to find Terrell and . . ."

Donavan stopped mid-sentence and began drooling.

"Donavan!" Penny yelled.

Penny could see that Donavan was trying to say something, but he could only make strange gurgling sounds. Donavan's eyes were wide with fear, looking all around the room. Saliva poured from his mouth, and he began biting down on his lip, causing it to bleed.

"Gggggg . . ."

Donavan's throat expanded suddenly, swelling as if someone were pumping air into it. After a few seconds of struggling against the pain, Donavan's throat collapsed on itself and shrank, leaving a thin neck no larger than a wrist with hundreds of pulsating veins in it. His eyes turned a purplish color and bulged slightly out of their sockets as a small stream of blood began dripping from the corners of his eyes. His tongue shot out of his mouth before he bit down, biting it in two.

"Terrell!" Penny screamed. "Where are you? Somebody, please help!"

Penny ran to her husband and lifted his head to see if he was still alive.

"Donavan!" Penny screamed. "Speak to me!"

Donavan gasped and suddenly opened his eyes. Penny watched in astonishment as his neck expanded, returning to normal. Donavan tried to talk but started coughing violently.

"It's okay, baby. Just relax, and I'll get help."

Penny lowered her husband's head to the floor and stood up to run when she froze. Standing in front of her was the child from the basement. Seeing the child shook Penny to her core, and she began slowly backing away from him.

"What do you want? Why are you here?"

The child kept moving toward Penny, his wide jet-black eyes reflecting her terrified face as he moved closer. His eyes were as black as night, like a world of cold, brutal evil was inside him. Penny shivered as she stared at the child, afraid the boy would send all the evil inside him to kill her and Donavan if she turned away.

"You don't love him," the child said in an icy whisper. "He is ours."

As the child moved closer, Penny became terrified at his appearance; his cheeks were large and puffy, while the rest of his body was frail and nothing but skin and bones. His head jerked spontaneously, causing him to struggle to maintain his balance as he walked. He contorted his body to avoid falling over, revealing the long thick vein that Penny had seen in the basement; the thick pulsating tube ran from between his shoulder blades, up his tiny neck, and into the base of his skull.

As Penny moved away from the boy, another equally terrifying child entered the room from the basement. And then another. And yet another. Soon the room was crowded with dozens of demon-like children, some growling while others were crying out as though in pain. Each child possessed some physical deformity: a little girl was missing half her scalp; a boy with a massive hole in the side of his face carried a toddler on his hip, the toddler growling and hissing, shoving its tiny fist into the hole in the boy's face. But they were all damaged children, seemingly tortured. And everyone had the same black marble eyes as the first child, empty yet filled with evil.

"What . . . what do you want?" whispered Penny through chattering teeth. None of the children responded. Instead, they all seemingly looked past her or through her as though they were looking into another world.

Suddenly, Penny recognized a distinct voice through the crying and growling.

"Mommy?" the voice called out. "Where are you?"

Penny's eyes widened, and she began searching the faces of the demonic children, looking for her son.

"Terrell, is that you?"

The tiny voice rang out once more.

"Mommy?"

"I'm here, baby. Where are you?"

As if sensing Penny's desire to locate her son, the large group of children made a path, and Penny saw her son. He was standing at the back of the room, plastered against the wall. His eyes were wild, and his mouth was foamy with saliva.

"John's here, Mom. I can't stop him."

Penny's eyes darted around the room, looking for the evil man that terrified her son.

"Where are you, you son of a bitch!" she screamed.

Suddenly, Terrell let out a wild scream and rushed toward Penny.

"Mommeeeee . . ." Terrell screamed as he sprinted through the group of children.

"Terrell!" Penny said happily, opening her arms to accept her son.

But their joy was but a brief moment. Terrell ran past his mother and launched himself upon his father. Penny screamed in horror as she watched her son rip mouthfuls of flesh from her husband's face.

"I'm sorry, Mommy," said Terrell between swallowing. "John said it's the only way to protect you."

Terrell continued feasting on his father's flesh, ripping out his ribcage and cracking the bones to suck out the marrow. He pulled out Donavan's heart, held it up for inspection, and shoved the muscle into the back of his throat, gagging as he tried to swallow it without chewing. The child vomited twice and hungrily slammed his face into the floor to suck up the putrid meat.

"So hungry . . . So hungry," Terrell repeated, licking the vomit. He spotted a piece of flesh that had slid across the floor, and he dove for it, thrusting his finger into his mouth and biting down hungrily, severing two of his fingers in the process. He smiled as the blood squirted from his two missing fingers and chewed until he consumed everything.

Suddenly he turned to Penny.

"It's the only way," Terrell whimpered.

Penny watched her son in a trance, unable to comprehend what she had witnessed.

"Terrell . . . Terrell . . ." she whispered repeatedly, her mind a scratched record stuck on repeat.

Terrell finished eating his father's corpse and tossed the remains aside. Still hungry, he gathered over his mother like a murderous storm cloud of uncontrolled rage, growling like an animal, unable and unwilling to stop himself from doing the unthinkable.

Penny's mind was gone. She didn't cry or scream when her son jumped upon her and bit into her breast; she could only whisper the sweetest name she'd ever known—Terrell.

3

Hearing and Knowing

The car stopped in front of the building, and Arlo watched as the students commiserated on the sidewalk. He was not in the mood for school today.

"Are you going to start your day by pouting?" asked Claire, putting the car in park.

Arlo ignored his mother and reached into the backseat to retrieve his schoolbag.

"Hey," Claire said as Arlo pretended to search for something in his backpack. "I'm talking to you."

Suddenly she grabbed her son's arm and pulled on it until he sat down.

"Arlo. Can you answer me?"

"No, Mom, I'm not pouting."

"Don't be like that."

"Like what?"

"You know how your dad gets when he drinks. He says a lot of dumb things he doesn't mean."

Arlo let his head fall back against the headrest and sighed.

"Do we have to talk about this now?"

"What you heard was the alcohol and nothing more."

Arlo looked at his mother and rolled his eyes.

"Really, Mom? The alcohol?"

"Yeah! It does strange things to people."

"So the alcohol made him tell you he wished you never had me?"

Claire's eyes widened.

"You heard that?"

"Who couldn't hear it? When you guys argue, the whole neighborhood knows."

"Look, Arlo. That was an argument between your dad's alcohol and my frustration with it."

"I know what I heard."

"Well . . ."

Claire stumbled to try to find the right words.

"When two people fight, sometimes they say the most hateful things to hurt one another. But it doesn't mean anything."

"So my feelings mean nothing?"

"No. . . . I mean, yes, of course, your feelings are important. You know what I mean."

"No, Mom, I don't."

"Your dad was angry because I poured out his beer, and he only said that stuff to piss me off."

"He says stuff about *me* to piss *you* off? Cool."

Claire softened her expression and caressed her son's face.

"I didn't realize you heard that, Arlo, and I'm sorry. You're right. There's no excuse for what he said. Just try to put it behind you. I'm certain he only said it because he was drunk."

Arlo opened the door and then turned to his mother.

"Drinking or not, he said it. And neither of you can unring that bell."

Arlo climbed out of the car and slammed the door. Just as he did, his best friend, Manuel, arrived.

"Hello, Mrs. Ortega," yelled Manuel to Arlo's mother.

"Hello, Mani," she replied. "How's your mom?"

"She just dropped me off. She's okay."

"Good."

Arlo grabbed Manuel's sleeve and pulled him along to the building. "Come on, let's go."

"Bye, Mrs. Ortega!"

Manuel tried waving to Arlo's mother, but she pulled away before he saw her.

"Jeez. What's going on? Are you in trouble or something?"

"Nah. Just parents being parents."

At that moment, a couple of boys bumped into Arlo from behind and knocked his bag to the ground. It was Nathan and Owen from the football team.

"King Dipshit and his lover," Nathan teased. "Why don't you two get a room or something?"

"Two fuckboys! What a couple of losers!" Owen chimed in.

Manuel was about to yell at the boys, but Arlo motioned for him to ignore them, and the two teens ran off. After the boys were gone, Manuel picked up his bag.

"Why do you let people pick on you like that, Arlo? You've got to stand up to those punks."

"It's best to ignore them. You saw what they did to Jared, didn't you?"

"Yeah, they beat him up. And?"

"This is high school, and we don't have time for childish stuff like that."

"That's dumb, Arlo. As my dad says, everyone has to take an ass beating sometimes. But you win when people learn they can't mess with you without a fight."

At that moment, the bell rang, and everyone started walking into the building.

"See you later, Mani. Same place at lunchtime?"

"Yeah. Same place."

"Cool. Later."

4

An Unwanted Audience

Arlo sat in homeroom, staring out the window, wishing he was in bed. As the teacher took roll, he replayed his parents' argument in his mind and could barely pay attention.

"Arlo," the teacher called.

But Arlo didn't hear him. He was too deep in thought, pitying himself for being such a weak person in his father's eyes.

"Arlo Ortega!" the teacher called again.

Arlo was deep into a fantasy about going away to college and never seeing his father again when he felt his chair move. He turned around to see a student, Jeff Blankenship, kicking his chair to get his attention. Jeff motioned to the teacher.

"Oh! I'm here!" Arlo quickly replied.

The teacher lowered his glasses and glared at Arlo.

"What's the matter? You don't know your name today? Did you leave your head on the pillow at home?"

Feeling embarrassed, Arlo looked away sheepishly as the classroom began giggling.

"Okay, that's enough," replied the teacher, shaking his head in disapproval before continuing with the roll call.

Arlo returned to thinking about his relationship with his family. His relationship with his father was awkward at best; they barely said more than hello when passing one another in the house. Arlo wanted to be closer to his dad, but he couldn't relate to anything about him. His father was chest-thumpingly macho—a man's man. Arlo's father was also the kind of man who expected his son to be immune to weakness. Arlo remembered when he was younger; he'd slammed his finger in a door and went to his father crying in pain.

"Why the hell are you crying? Stop acting like a pussy."

Although Arlo was very young, his father's words stayed with him forever. He never saw him the same after that. To Arlo, he became a permanent beer-chugging brute who overrode common sense to support his caveman mentality—even at the expense of his family.

Meanwhile, Arlo went out of his way to be the exact opposite of his father. He became reserved and quiet—he was respectful of others and rarely displayed anger. On the advice of his mother, Arlo found poetry. He began digging into his emotions, fears, and dreams. He shunned sports and developed a fondness for soft music—sounds his father hated. But Arlo didn't care.

One day he attempted to give his father an indirect exorcism by blasting jazz music. After yelling and cursing about "that goddamned racket," his father went out onto the porch and drank until he passed out, a hilarious yet satisfying moment that Arlo cherished. The gulf between their two personalities couldn't be more significant.

Finally, the bell rang, and everyone began exiting the classroom. As Arlo stood to file out behind the others, he looked outside and saw something peculiar—a girl standing on the school lawn, staring at him with wide, unblinking eyes. Their eyes met, and Arlo quickly looked away. Pretending not to notice her, he grabbed his bag from the floor and slung it on his shoulder before looking outside again. But this time, the girl was gone.

Arlo went on to his first-period class and thought nothing of the interaction. Most of his day was uneventful until his English Literature class ended. He saw the girl again when he walked into the hallway with the other students, and this time she stared at him between groups of students buzzing past her. As Arlo walked quickly toward the girl, she became evasive, dipping in and out of the crowd to make eye contact before disappearing and popping up in another part of the hall. When he finally arrived at his class, Arlo turned and waited for the girl to reappear—but she never did. Feeling frustrated, Arlo entered the classroom and took his seat.

5 |

The Bleachers

It was lunchtime, and Arlo was sitting on the bleachers, waiting for his friend, Manuel, to arrive when he looked up and saw a girl walking across the field toward him. Arlo became uncomfortable as she approached. He tried writing in his book of poems, but his nervousness made his hands shake, and he had to put his pen away. Who was this girl, and what did she want with him? She seemed to appear out of nowhere, and that frightened Arlo. He felt invaded by the girl's presence, like someone forcing themselves onto an already crowded bus.

"You wanna go out on a date?" the girl immediately asked when she arrived.

"We don't even know each other," Arlo finally said.

"Sure we do," the girl replied. "You're Arlo, and I'm Isadora."

"Uh-huh," replied Arlo, shading his eyes to look at the boys playing baseball.

"So . . . are we going out or what?"

Arlo intentionally dropped his book on the bench and took his time retrieving it. But Isadora didn't turn away—her glare only intensified as she sat waiting for Arlo's response. She walked over and sat on the bench next to him. After squirming for a few moments, Arlo replied in a very soft tone.

"I guess."

Isadora leaned back on her elbows and put her sneakers on the bleachers. Arlo watched nervously as the tomboy casually produced a pack of cigarettes from her jeans, ripped open the package with her teeth, pulled out a cigarette, and lit it.

"Yeah? So that means you're my boyfriend now, right?" she asked, making a circle with her mouth and puffing out rings of smoke.

Arlo squirmed in his seat once more. Why did Isadora choose him? Was this a joke? If she was from his school, and he wasn't sure she was, surely she knew his reputation and how the other boys often referred to him as KD (King Dipshit). The name didn't bother him much because it was the name the sports-crazed jocks assigned him when they found out he loved poems. The girls in school were less brutal, but only slightly; they laughed and whispered whenever the jocks played their cruel jokes and spoke of Arlo as the "nerdy kid." But none of the girls expressed interest in him—until now.

"Well?" asked Isadora impatiently.

Arlo blinked his eyes and came back to reality.

"Well, what?"

"Are you my boyfriend or not?"

The word *boyfriend* sounded strange in association with Arlo's name, and he didn't know how to handle it. He smiled uncomfortably and quickly looked away.

"Yeah," he finally responded. "And are you my girlfriend?"

Isadora chuckled and took a long final drag on her cigarette before flicking it away.

"No fucking shit, genius," she replied. The words were so crass that Arlo winced at the vulgarity—the curse words vandalized the moment like fingernails running across a chalkboard.

Arlo stared at the short, brown-haired girl from head to toe. Visually, there was nothing cute about Isadora. Her nails were short like she gnawed at them constantly. Her clothing screamed the boys' section at the local department store, from her shirt to her shoes. Isadora's chapped lips were red—not from lipstick but from her habit of peeling the dried skin off her lips.

Isadora's personality was even more unappealing. She walked around with a gigantic chip on her shoulder, daring anyone to knock it off. There was no filter between her thoughts and mouth—she said what she meant to say, and to hell with anyone with a lower rank than a parent or teacher who said something about it. When Isadora spoke, she often sounded and moved with the mannerisms of a teenaged boy, which threw Arlo off. In many ways, the girl seemed to be more masculine than him. She even smoked cigarettes, something Arlo wanted to do but had never dared to try. Isadora's masculine swagger was so intense that Arlo wouldn't have been surprised if Isadora had dropped her pants to reveal two gigantic testicles.

Still, something underneath Isadora's armor made him say yes to her, something beautiful that he had never recognized until she crossed the field and sat next to him. There was a quiet softness beneath her brown eyes, a vulnerability she did her best to hide but couldn't. Arlo didn't know if his sensing of fragility in Isadora was because she wanted him to see it or because he also was a delicate soul, seeking kinship in a world filled with noise. All he knew was Isadora chose him to reveal herself to, and he accepted.

Arlo had never had a girlfriend before and wondered about the next step. Isadora didn't strike him as the type of girl to hold hands, but they could eat lunch together sometimes. Sure, they'd probably catch hell from the other kids, but that was the wonderful thing about misery—the company.

"Let me see your hand," barked Isadora.

"What?" asked Arlo in disbelief.

"Don't be a chicken shit. Let me see it," Isadora repeated.

Arlo nervously extended his hand to Isadora and watched in surprise as she took his hand and held it.

"I've liked you for a long time."

"Really?"

"Ever since middle school."

"Middle school? Did I know you then?"

"Shit, dude. You must have scrambled eggs for brains. Don't you remember me? We were in the same homeroom."

"Mr. Jackson's class? You were there?"

"Um, duh! I sat a couple of seats behind you."

Arlo racked his brain, trying to remember the people in his seventh-grade homeroom, but all he could think about was Isadora holding his hand. Although her nails were dirty, Isadora's hand was much softer than it appeared.

Suddenly Isadora stood and shaded her eyes to look at a large group of girls walking on the far end of the baseball field. She quickly turned and grabbed her books from the bench.

"Hey, I need to go. The Rich Bitch Patrol is heading our way, and I got into a fight with one of them a few days back. One more incident and I'm toast. I'll see you later, okay?"

"Wait. Shouldn't we exchange phone numbers or something?"

"Sure. Do you have something to write with?"

Arlo searched his bookbag but could not locate the pen he'd just been using.

"Shit, dude. You're more unorganized than me."

Isadora reached into her back pocket and pulled out a small switch-blade. Surprised, Arlo took a step back and stared at the black-handled weapon.

"You carry a knife?"

With a flick of the wrist, Isadora opened the knife.

"You never know when you're going to need it."

Isadora stuck out her index finger and ran the knife across, causing blood to bubble up.

"Give me a piece of paper."

Unable to take his eyes off the girl's wound, Arlo reached into his bag and retrieved a blank piece of notebook paper. He watched in shock as Isadora bit her lip and wrote seven numbers with her blood. When she finished, she smiled and inspected the bloody note with pride.

"Fuck pens, right?"

Isadora stuck her bloody finger into her mouth and sucked the blood off. Afterward, she handed the paper to Arlo, and he took it by one of the corners, afraid he would smudge the numbers.

"I'm usually home by ten or so."

"Ten? That's late, isn't it?"

"For who, some candy-assed bookworm?"

"I mean, won't your parents complain?"

"What parents?"

The question startled Arlo, and he eyed the girl curiously. Did she mean she lived alone?

Isadora held the knife to Arlo, and he looked at her, confused.

"What?" he asked, terrified by what his new girlfriend wanted him to do.

"Aren't you going to give me your number?" she asked.

Arlo looked at the drop of blood on the blade's edge and started searching through his bag again.

"I'm sure I brought a pen with me. Let me just . . ."

Isadora burst into laughter.

"What? Don't tell me you're such a pussy you won't even cut your finger. No way!"

Embarrassed, Arlo took the knife from Isadora and stared at the blade. The knife looked like a gigantic sword in his hands. He didn't like weapons. Too many things could go wrong. Still, he didn't want to seem like a coward to Isadora, especially since she'd already sliced her finger like it was nothing. Arlo placed the blade on his finger and looked away. When he pulled the knife across his hand, he felt a stinging pain, like when he got pinched by a crab at the beach. Arlo looked down at the wound and was shocked—the cut was worse than he expected. Unlike Isadora's injury, which left a small, neat line of blood, Arlo could see the inside of his finger; the meat looked puffy and white, like his finger had cotton inside. The wound filled with dark red blood within seconds and began pouring steadily from his finger.

"Shit, dude," Isadora exclaimed with a tinge of worry. "Be careful. You almost cut your finger off."

Arlo grabbed a fresh piece of paper and scribbled his phone number in blood, grimacing while the open wound widened with each stroke. After finishing writing the numbers, he gave the paper to Isadora. Arlo cupped the injured finger in his other hand and squeezed hard to stop the bleeding while Isadora watched with an annoyed look.

"Here, let me help you."

Isadora pulled out the lining of her jeans pocket and used the knife to cut it out. She expertly sliced the lining into two thin pieces.

"What are you doing?"

"You'd probably die if I weren't here," she replied. "Such a baby. Here, give me your finger."

Suddenly Isadora moved close and took Arlo's bloody hand in hers.

"If you tell anyone I did this, I'll kick your ass."

Isadora lifted Arlo's bloody finger to her mouth and sucked hard, causing pain to shoot through Arlo's finger.

"Hey! Ow!" Arlo said, and winced.

"Come on, man," Isadora mumbled with his finger still in her mouth. "Stop being a baby."

Soon Arlo couldn't feel the pain in his finger anymore—the stinging replaced by the warmth of Isadora's tongue as she moved it up and down the wound. When Isadora removed the digit from her mouth, the blood was gone. She quickly placed a piece of the pocket lining on the injury and used the other piece of cloth as a tourniquet to stop the bleeding. Finally, Isadora spat the blood on the ground.

"Don't worry, that's a baby cut. You'll live," said Isadora, tucking the paper with Arlo's phone number into her jeans.

Arlo couldn't believe his eyes. Who was this girl, and why was she so wild?

"Make sure you go to the nurse and get something to put on that cut. Infection is a bitch."

Arlo didn't know how to respond, so he gave the only response that came to his mind.

"Uh-huh."

Isadora grabbed her books and smiled at Arlo before walking away.

"Call me tonight," she yelled back. "I'll be home."

6

Arlo and Manuel

Arlo and Manuel got off the bus and started walking to their houses.

"She came up to you out of nowhere?"

"Yeah. I was sitting on the bench, waiting for you to show up. Where were you?"

"Sorry, dude. I had to take a dump."

"Too much information, Mani."

"Well, I did. Anyway . . . Did she ask you out? Just like that?"

"I couldn't believe it. It was weird."

"Seriously."

"She told me her name was Isadora and that she sat behind me in Mr. Jackson's homeroom in middle school."

"I was there, and I don't remember her. Isadora? What's her last name?"

Arlo frowned.

"I didn't ask."

Manuel took a box of gummy bears from his backpack, shook out a few, and gave the rest to Arlo.

"Well, I never heard of anyone named Isadora in our classes, and you and I have been friends since the third grade."

"I couldn't think of anyone by that name, either."

Suddenly a devilish grin flickered across Manuel's face.

"How does she look? Is she hot?"

"What do you mean?"

"You know, is she smashable? Does she have big tits?"

Arlo blushed slightly and looked into the empty box of gummy bears.

"You got any more of these?" he asked, avoiding Manuel's question.

Manuel stepped in front of Arlo and stopped walking.

"Aw, come on, bro. Don't be all shy now."

Arlo moved around his friend and continued walking.

"I'm not shy. I wasn't thinking about that."

Manuel shook his head in disbelief.

"Bro, you agreed to date a girl, and you can't even describe how she looks? She must be a real wildebeest."

Feeling a little offended, Arlo snapped at his friend.

"At least she looks better than your girlfriend. How much does Tammy weigh now, three hundred pounds?"

Manuel's face turned serious, and he angrily spat out his gummy bears.

"Tammy has a medical condition, so fuck you."

Arlo chuckled a bit and continued walking. He knew what to say to make Manuel angry.

"Fuck you right back. Don't talk about my girl, and I won't talk about yours."

"Now she's your girl? You don't even know her."

"Nobody knows anyone when they first meet, do they?"

"Okay, facts. But you may want to ask around about that girl to find out if she's psycho or something. The whole situation seems weird."

The duo arrived at Manuel's house and watched as Maria, Manuel's kid sister, ran to unlock the gate.

"Hey, Maria!" Arlo said in greeting.

"Hi, Arlo! You going to show me how to ride my bike today?"

"I can't ride bikes today because I have a lot of homework. Maybe this weekend?"

Manuel rudely interrupted by pushing the little girl away from the gate and walking into the yard.

"Stop being a pest!" he barked at his sister.

Annoyed, Maria stuck out her tongue and stumbled back.

"Mom's mad at you because you didn't clean your room, and I'm the one that told her about it," sneered Maria.

"Get lost, loser! Wait until I get a hold of that doll of yours. I'll rip off her head, and you won't be able to find it for a week."

"You'd better leave my things alone! I'm going to tell Mom!"

Maria took off running into the house while Manuel turned back to Arlo.

"Are you going to call that girl tonight?"

"I don't know. Maybe."

"Well, this time, ask for her complete name."

"Yeah. See you tomorrow."

7

The Call

When the phone rang, Arlo was about to shove a spoonful of his mother's world-famous cheddar mashed potatoes into his mouth.

"Who could that be?" asked Claire.

"I'll get it," piped up Arlo.

"You sit right there and finish eating. You act like you pay the bills around here or something," replied Arlo's father before anyone else could get out of their chair.

Jaime walked over to the phone and answered it.

"Hello?"

Arlo looked nervously at his father and then at his mother before lowering his head in embarrassment.

"Yeah, Arlo's home, but he's eating dinner now. . . . Yes . . . okay. I'll let him know you called. Isadora, is it? Sure thing. Does he have your number? Okay, I'll let him know. Bye."

Jaime hung up the phone and turned to face Arlo with a big smile.

"Isadora, huh?"

Arlo's face became redder.

"It's nothing, Dad. We're just completing a homework assignment together."

Claire smiled and chimed in.

"You have a girlfriend? I think that's wonderful. It will help if you read some of your poetry. Girls like that stuff!"

"No, Mom. She's just a classmate."

"Isadora's a beautiful name. Where does she live?"

"Gosh! Would you guys stop?"

Arlo took a final bite of his mashed potatoes and tried drowning out the voices of his annoying parents by gulping a glass of water.

"It's about time you got a girlfriend," continued Jaime. "You're about to be sixteen this year, and having a girlfriend is better than wasting your time on video games with that goddamned boy up the street."

"I want to meet Isadora. Why don't you invite her over this weekend?" asked Claire.

Arlo sighed and stood to clear the table.

"I told you, she's not my girlfriend. Just a friend!"

Jaime walked back to the table and sat down to finish his dinner.

"There are two things about this girl you need to remember. First, make sure you never tell her you love her, and second, never let her know you care too much."

Arlo's mother quickly protested.

"Jaime! That's horrible!"

"But it's true. Girls turn into monsters when they learn they have you by the balls."

Arlo quickly exited the dining room, put the dishes into the kitchen sink, and went to his room. Slamming his door shut, he flopped down on his bed. Slowly his frown melted away and revealed an enormous smile. Although Arlo told his parents he didn't have a girlfriend, he was happy to finally have one. He saw how the couples in school held hands and rode the bus together. A relationship was something Arlo longed to experience. Since entering high school, there had been four school dances, and he avoided attending them. Now he would have Isadora as a partner.

Arlo took a deep breath and picked up the phone. After digging in his pocket for the bloody piece of paper, he pulled it out and dialed

Isadora's number. He looked at his injured index finger as the phone rang, and he smiled.

"Weird," Arlo whispered as he remembered Isadora sucking the blood from his finger. Still, he saw the romance in what his new girlfriend strangely did for him. She cared about Arlo without even knowing that much about him. His finger ached when he bent it, but he could forgive that discomfort for the new memory he now shared with Isadora.

Arlo stayed on the phone, waiting for Isadora to answer, but she never picked up. Frustrated and confused, he hung up and laid down on his bed. Thinking about the day's events a few moments more, he pulled out his pad and pen to write a poem—about Isadora.

8

Our Son, The Poet

Jaime laid in bed, watching his wife apply lotion to her hands as she sat in front of the mirror. Frustrated with how slowly she was moving, he grabbed the remote control and turned on the TV.

"What are you doing?" asked Claire while wrapping her hair in her silk bonnet. "You know I need to get up early tomorrow for that big team meeting."

Jaime ignored her and flipped through the channels.

"Jaime! Come on, turn it off. I need some sleep."

"Not from what I see. You're sitting in front of that mirror like you're planning to be awake all night."

Claire began applying a mud mask to her face.

"You know, Arlo heard what you said during our argument."

"What did I say?"

Claire looked at her husband incredulously.

"You don't remember saying you wished he wasn't born?"

"Bullshit. I never said such a thing."

"You did, and he heard you."

"Well, if I did, it's your fault."

"What?"

"That's right! Who told you to pour out my beer?"

"That's beside the point, Jaime. Arlo heard what you said, and I think you need to apologize to him because his feelings are hurt."

"That's fucking ridiculous. Arlo needs to grow up."

"*He* needs to grow up?"

"That's goddamned right. Pussyfooting around this world will not get him shit, and nobody gives two good goddamns about his feelings."

"I don't believe you, Jaime. So you're not going to apologize?"

"Nope. I didn't say it to him, so I have no reason to say sorry. If anything, he needs to apologize to me for eavesdropping on an adult conversation. Goddamned kids."

"I'm not going to argue with you tonight, Jaime. I guess I know how you feel about Arlo having a girlfriend."

Jaime stopped turning the channels and started watching football.

"It's okay," he replied.

"Just okay?" asked Claire.

Claire slid into bed next to Jaime, mud covering most of her face.

"It's about time for him to like girls, isn't it?"

Claire shrugged.

"I agree. I'm just a little shocked."

"At what?"

"Arlo's not into sports. Poetry is his thing, and he's a bit of a loner regarding his art."

"Complete bullshit."

"So . . . he's talented. Have you read any of his poetry? Our son's going to be an academic, no doubt about it. And those types usually have a different perspective on love than most boys his age."

Jaime turned to look at his wife.

"What? Gay?"

"Calm down and put your gaydar away. Arlo's into girls, especially ones with big racks."

Jaime laughed.

"That's my boy! Hell yeah! How do you know that?"

"I'm his mom, remember? Nobody can hide anything from me in this house. I was cleaning his bedroom and found a couple of girlie magazines underneath his mattress. And now, with the phone call from that Isadora girl, I think you can rest your ancient caveman's brain and breathe a sigh of relief."

"That doesn't necessarily confirm anything. It's still early. The true test will be what happens when Arlo's away at college."

Claire playfully removed mud from her face with her index finger and wiped it on her husband's cheek.

"It doesn't matter. Straight or gay, we'll love our son the same."

Annoyed, Jaime wiped the mud off his cheek.

"You women and your damned beauty products."

"Aw, is the baby mad now?"

Claire leaned over and kissed her husband gently on the lips. While he was distracted, she snatched the TV remote control from him and hit the off button.

"Hey, I was watching that."

"Not tonight, sir. We're going to sleep."

After placing the remote out of Jaime's reach, Claire turned off the lamp and laid down. Jaime registered his disapproval by grumbling before turning away from his wife and closing his eyes. Within a few seconds, they both drifted off to sleep.

Neither of them noticed the tall, slender figure standing outside their window. It was a teenage girl; her youthful face was so beautiful that the darkness made her features seem angelic.

Suddenly there was a noise from the street, and an approaching car drove past the house, shining its bright headlights on the girl. She looked at the vehicle and hissed at the intrusion; the car's headlights revealed a terrifying truth—while the teenager had been a girl at one point, she was no longer human. It was a monster—a demon tortured and twisted into existence through pain. One of its breasts was exposed to the night air, a massive chunk missing, showing the cartilage within its chest cavity. Its ribcage was open to the crisp night wind, exposing organs rendered useless to the creature when it became a servant of hell. The ghostly demon was a creature whose soul was missing—taken or possibly given to whoever mastered the tools of suffering. No humanity or emotion was left, and its jet-black eyes bore the confirmation of such truths. It was a soulless creature filled only with the insatiable desire to please its master.

The monster turned away from the road and continued staring at the couple with wide black eyes. Soon thick drool poured from its mouth, and drops of sweat formed on its pale, leathery skin. The remaining bowels within its stomach began twisting back and forth like angry worms, emitting a low growling sound, and the creature started biting and grinding its teeth. It could smell the flesh of the couple—their insides and the fermented liquids bubbling within their intestines. It wanted to devour them. The beast began trembling as it yearned to take the couple. It moved closer to the window, placed its pale, cold palm on the glass, and shook uncontrollably until the glass shattered.

Jaime sat up in the darkness and looked around the room.

"What the hell?" he asked, reaching underneath his bed to retrieve his gun case. His wife grabbed his arm and held on tight.

"What is it?" she whispered. Jaime removed Claire's hand from his arm and unlocked his gun case. He leapt over his wife with his pistol in hand and ran to turn on the bedroom lights. After spotting the broken glass, he tiptoed to the window and peered out into the night—nothing was there.

9

Like Melting Ice in the Sun

Arlo was restless. Isadora hadn't returned any of his calls, and he hadn't seen her in school. He tried to remain calm by telling himself she would reach out in time, but he became nervous after the first day of silence. Where had Isadora gone? Was she sick? Why hadn't she answered his calls?

On the second day of her absence, Arlo roamed the school hallways, scanning the approaching faces, hoping to see his girlfriend—but he never saw her. When that didn't work, he started asking around the school, sometimes pretending to be a messenger sent by a teacher to deliver a message, other times peppering students with questions. But no one saw her or even knew Isadora by name.

On the third day, Arlo was a bundle of nerves. He sat in Algebra class, shifting uncomfortably in his seat, his eyes alternating between the clock and each passerby in the hallway. Occasionally depression set in, and his spirits dipped so low that Arlo resigned to the possibility that Isadora played a joke on him, recruited by an anonymous group of pranksters out for a quick laugh at his expense. But then the cut on his finger began to itch, and he remembered the day on the baseball field, and he thought, *There's no way she was playing.*

Arlo looked at the clock with a frustration he'd never felt before. He tried to do one of the math problems but repeatedly wrote his girlfriend's name on his paper. Angry with his inability to focus, Arlo lifted his finger and looked at the wound—it was healing nicely, just as Isadora had said it would. Slowly he began peeling the scab off the injury, hoping the sight of fresh blood would bring about Isadora's return and save him from his world of suffering.

"Where is she?" Arlo whispered.

The teacher called on him twice to answer a math problem, and Arlo declined to answer twice. Instead, he focused his mental energy on making the clock move faster.

Suddenly a thought came into Arlo's head, and he smiled.

"The baseball field! Why didn't I think of it before?" he whispered. By the time the bell rang for lunch, Arlo was in such a state that he pushed several students away from the classroom door and sprinted to the baseball field.

When Arlo arrived at the diamond, his heart sank; Isadora wasn't there. Instead, two boys and two girls occupied the benches. Arlo didn't recognize the girls, but the two rowdy boys he knew instantly—Owen and Nathan, the boys who bullied him at every opportunity. Arlo quickly tried to turn around and make his getaway before anyone saw him, but he was too slow. Owen saw Arlo and began the bullying.

"Hey, fellas, look who showed up. King Dipshit!"

Arlo turned around to face the group and remained silent.

"No fucking way!" chimed in Owen's friend, Nathan. "Dipshit, why are you here? Did you come to hang out with the in-crowd?"

"Not with those clothes," piped up one of the girls.

"What the hell is he wearing?" asked her friend.

Arlo walked to the far end of the bleachers and sat down. Owen rushed over and sat beside him as soon as he did.

"You're a born loser, aren't you?"

Owen grabbed the collar of Arlo's shirt and yanked it.

"Look at these hand-me-downs you're wearing. This fucking shirt looks like you wear it at least four times a week. And these no-name shoes? Fuck! I'll bet if you tried to run, the soles would come off. You're a complete dipshit."

Arlo ignored the comments and took out his book of poetry. As he started reading, Nathan walked over and stood before the boy.

"Whatcha reading, Dipshit?"

Nathan snatched the book out of Arlo's hand.

"Hey! Give it back!"

"Let's see what you're reading."

Arlo was shaking with rage. He stood and tried grabbing the book away from Nathan.

"If you don't give that back, I'll . . ."

Nathan held the book high above his head.

"You'll do what?"

Arlo tried thinking of a threat to move the boy to action, but the more he struggled to grab his book, the more he realized he'd never get it back. He looked over at the two girls; they laughed at the bullying. Suddenly a wicked thought came to Arlo, and he smiled.

"What will I do? I'll tell everyone about your gonorrhea problem."

Nathan stopped laughing.

"Wait, what did you say?"

"I'll let everyone know you're burning!"

The statement got the attention of the two girls, and they looked at one another with confused looks on their faces.

"What did he say?" one of the girls asked.

"Nathan didn't tell you, did he? He's got the clap. Ask Coach Thompson if you don't believe me."

Nathan's face turned red, and the book fell to the ground.

"Now, you take that back."

"I can't. It's true."

Owen took a step away from his friend and eyed him suspiciously.

"Is that true?"

Nathan started stuttering as he tried to explain.

"It's . . . I mean, no way! That prick's lying!"

Arlo intensified his attack.

"It's not a lie. Ask Coach Thompson. Why would I need to make up a lie like that? Nathan's burning!"

One of the girls stood and yelled at Nathan.

"Oh my God! I kissed you!"

Nathan held up a fist and waved it at Arlo.

"That fucker's lying! He's making it up! I promise!" Nathan yelled.

"You know it's not a lie!" replied Arlo.

Suddenly one of the girls stood and pointed to Nathan's pants.

"W-what the hell is that?"

Everyone turned their attention to Nathan's khaki pants.

"Is that . . . blood?" asked Arlo. He couldn't believe what he was seeing. There was a red stain on Nathan's crotch.

Embarrassed and unsure of what to say, Nathan became silent, his face twisted as he searched for an explanation. He looked down at the front of his pants and rubbed the red stain.

"It's not what you think. I was in the cafeteria, and it might be the . . ."

"Dude! Look at his pants! It's getting bigger!" yelled Arlo. "You *are* sick!"

The students watched the tiny red dot on Nathan's khaki pants grow and spread down his legs.

"Shit!" yelled Owen.

"Oh my God! I think I'm going to be sick," yelled one of the girls. She grabbed her friend by the hand, and the two girls took off running across the field toward the school.

Nathan moaned and grabbed his pants.

"I-I'm going to get y-you," he said to Arlo and ran toward the school. As Arlo and Owen watched the boy running across the field, both remained quiet for a few moments. Finally, Owen spoke.

"How did you know?" asked Owen.

The question was just as confusing to Arlo as seeing Nathan's blood. Unable to respond, he looked briefly at Owen and then watched the field.

"You'd better see if your friend made it to the nurse's office," replied Arlo. After searching Arlo's face, Owen turned and ran across the field.

"That was wild," whispered a voice from the bushes behind the bleachers. Arlo turned to see Isadora step out of her hiding place.

"You," said Arlo, trying to mask the excitement in his voice. "Where have you been?"

"Minding my fucking business. You?"

"I called you."

"I called you first."

"Why didn't you return my calls?"

Isadora walked over and sat next to Arlo.

"Do you think this is the fifties or something? I don't bake cakes, and I'm damn sure not sitting by the phone waiting on some guy to return my call. You snooze, you lose."

Before Arlo could respond, Isadora pulled him close and planted a kiss on his lips.

"You miss me, baby?" she asked. Flustered by the sudden display of emotion, Arlo smiled and gave the only response he could.

"Y-yeah."

Isadora smiled and kissed Arlo again, shoving her tongue into his mouth. The act surprised Arlo even more than the initial kiss, and he recoiled.

"Hey, hold on."

"What, you never French kissed before?"

"No . . . I mean, um, yeah. I mean, it's been a long time."

Isadora laughed and stood up to look at the field.

"He deserved that, you know."

"Who? Nathan?"

"I mean, who does he think he is to walk around this school bullying people? People like him need a lesson in pain."

"Today, I think Nathan learned his lesson. I doubt he'll be bullying anyone anytime soon."

"You mean the blood on his pants?"

"Yeah."

"That was child's play. He's not hurt at all—it's a mental trick I played on him."

Arlo stood and moved closer to Isadora.

"What are you saying? That was you?"

"It was a gag that I learned. Nathan's not hurt; he has Kool-Aid on his pants."

Arlo burst into laughter.

"Are you serious? Was that a joke? Wow! Remind me never to get on your bad side."

Isadora turned to look into Arlo's eyes. She wasn't smiling.

"One day, everyone must learn the truth about pain—that there is nothing and everything in what it does. Only a few know the truth— real pain is delicious, like bruised blackberries in the evening sun, or ice melting on warm pavement. Pain walks hand in hand with pleasure. For those that deny the exquisite beauty of it all, they are all blind children, naked and stumbling through a world filled with poisonous lies. They deny themselves of pleasure."

Isadora's words scared Arlo, and he took a step away from her.

"Wait. You said that was a joke, right? Nathan's not hurt, is he?"

Suddenly Isadora grabbed Arlo and wrapped her arms around him, planting a new kiss on his lips.

"I'm in love with you, Arlo. Do you love me?"

Arlo tried to look away, but Isadora grabbed his face and turned it back to hers.

"Do you love me?"

"Y-yes."

"I want to show you something."

"What is it?"

"Meet me at the Bradley Museum at midnight tonight."

"What's at the museum?"

"There's something special I want to show you."

"I don't know. My parents would never let me go out that late."

"Obviously. Sneak out."

"Sneak out? I've never done that before."

Isadora pushed Arlo and turned away from him.

"You're a fucking liar."

"What? I'm not!"

"You're just like all the others. Pretending to love but never trusting anyone. I'm sorry I even met you."

Arlo moved close and wrapped his arms around Isadora.

"Look. I'm sorry. I'll meet you, okay?"

"You're a fuckboy! Get away from me, loser!"

"Calm down, Isadora. I love you. I'll meet you there, okay?"

Isadora turned back to face him.

"Don't play with me."

"I'm not. I'll be there."

"Don't stand me up. I would never forgive you if you did that to me."

"I won't."

10

Someone's Lying

"Did you hear what happened to Nathan Cooper?"

Arlo turned to see Manuel running up to the bus, breathing heavily. Both boys boarded the bus, walked to the rear, and sat down.

"Three more minutes, and you would've been calling your parents for a ride home. Why were you late for the bus?"

"I was playing a basketball game of twenty-one with Craig Hollis. Forget that. Did you hear about Nathan?"

"Yeah, I heard."

"Word around the school is that he got stabbed."

Arlo smiled. His lie had morphed into something different since he'd last seen Nathan sprinting toward the school building.

"You don't say."

"Yeah. Everyone's saying Nathan's girlfriend caught him cheating and stabbed him in the genitals."

"You believe that?"

"I don't know. But two girls are mouthing off about seeing him bleeding."

"They're saying they saw his girlfriend stab him? Really?"

"That's what John told me in English class. I know, right? It's probably a bullshit story."

"I saw him when he first started bleeding."

"No shit!"

"We were at the baseball field when it happened."

"You saw him get stabbed?"

"Nobody stabbed him. We all saw a dot on the front of his pants, which then got bigger. He ran to find the nurse before we knew what was happening."

"Gosh!"

"Tell me about it."

"Well, whatever happened, he's in the hospital now."

Arlo laughed and shook his head in disagreement.

"Nah. Nathan's not in the hospital. Somebody gave you some jacked-up information."

"What do you mean?"

"He's not even sick. I saw him running toward the school with Kool-Aid on his pants."

"Kool-Aid?"

"Yeah. Nathan wasn't bleeding. It was a practical joke someone played on him with Kool-Aid packs."

Manuel's face grew serious.

"That wasn't Kool-Aid, Arlo. That was blood."

"Whatever. You don't know what you're talking about."

"I'm not lying. It was blood because I saw it smeared on the hall floor in front of the computer lab."

Arlo turned to look at Manuel's face, and saw that his friend wasn't joking.

"It wasn't blood," Arlo whispered, trying to convince himself. "I'm sure of it."

Manuel shrugged and sat back in the seat.

"All I know is that the ambulance came and took him to the hospital."

Arlo leaned against the bus window and watched the buildings pass in a blur. Isadora told him it was all a joke, but now he wasn't so sure. Although he'd been sitting in front of Nathan when the blood appeared, Arlo couldn't be sure Isadora hadn't injured Nathan with some weapon.

"Hey, was your girl in school today?"

"Yeah, I spoke to Isadora."

"Did you get her last name?"

"Not yet. I didn't have time."

"Who's her homeroom teacher?"

Arlo frowned.

"Hey, man. Why do you keep asking me so many questions about Isadora?"

"I don't know. That name is weird."

"So, you don't like her name. Big fucking deal. I don't know if you realize it, but my name's weird, too."

"It's not just that. I went into the principal's office and asked about her."

"You did? Why the hell did you do that?"

"It turns out the school *never* had a student under that name. Ever."

"That doesn't mean anything."

"She could've given you a fake name."

"I'll ask her about it. I'm meeting her tonight."

"What do you mean?"

"I'm sneaking out to meet her at midnight."

Manuel became nervous.

"I don't know, man. Maybe you should get to know Isadora better."

"She's a girl, Manuel, not a killer."

"But you don't know anything about her—you don't know her name, what classes she takes, or the kinds of friends she has."

"You're in no position to judge me. How often have you snuck out of the house to see your girlfriend?"

"And that's the thing! You don't *know* my girlfriend, Tammy, but you *know* her friends and her family. You know what classes she takes. With this Isadora girl, you don't know shit, and neither does anyone else. Doesn't that make you a little suspicious?"

"Maybe. But that's why we're going out tonight."
"I wouldn't go if I were you."
"Well, thank God you're not me. Mind your business."

11

Through the Night

Arlo tiptoed through the dark house, inched open the front door, and snuck out. As he walked across the front yard, he continuously looked back at the upstairs windows to see if any lights suddenly turned on. Satisfied that his parents didn't hear his exit, Arlo started jogging.

Arlo hadn't taken three steps when a voice called out to him.

"Hey!"

Arlo spun around and almost fell to the ground. It was Isadora.

"Where did you come from?"

"I've been waiting outside your house for an hour. You ready?"

Arlo stared at Isadora in disbelief. He didn't recognize the girl standing before him. Unlike the other times Arlo had seen her, Isadora's appearance was gothic; she wore black makeup, and her hair was oily. Instead of the jeans and T-shirt he'd previously seen her wear, Isadora wore a black jacket and black leather pants. Isadora's appearance gave Arlo second thoughts. He remembered what Manuel told him about waiting, and regretted not taking the advice. The girl standing before Arlo wasn't Isadora; this girl seemed to be a witch.

"Are you ready or not?" Isadora asked once more.

"I guess," Arlo replied reluctantly.

Isadora pointed to the forest.

"Let's go this way."

"The forest? Are you kidding me?"

"Don't be such a pussy."

"I'm not going through that forest. I live around here, remember? I know there are more than a few wild animals in there."

Isadora grabbed Arlo's hand and tried to pull him toward the forest.

"We don't have all night. Let's go."

But Arlo was firm and pulled back.

"I said no."

Annoyed, Isadora stamped her foot and took off walking.

"Fine, we'll take the long route!"

As the two began walking on the street, Arlo saw his opportunity to learn more about his girlfriend.

"What's your last name?"

"Are you serious?"

"Yeah. You never told me your last name."

"Does it matter?"

"To me, yes. If we're in a relationship, we should know more about each other."

Isadora remained quiet as they walked. Frustrated by her wall of silence, Arlo pushed again.

"You're not going to tell me your last name?"

Suddenly Isadora stopped walking.

"Tell that dumbass, Manuel, to mind his goddamned business."

The statement surprised Arlo, and he feigned innocence.

"Manuel? What are you talking about?"

Isadora moved close to Arlo and shoved her finger into his face.

"Don't insult my intelligence. I know you and that prick talk about me. Just because I don't walk around school running my mouth, don't think I'm some dumb chick. The two of you act like a couple of bitches. Do you and Manuel have sleepovers and pillow fights, too?"

Isadora turned away from Arlo and continued walking. Offended and a little angry by his girlfriend's sharp tongue, Arlo thought about giving Isadora a dose of her own medicine by saying something insulting. But seeing how angry Isadora became, he decided to drop the subject and walked on in silence.

Finally, the two teens arrived at the museum.

"It's beautiful, isn't it?" asked Isadora, her eyes locked in a dreamy gaze on the building draped in shadow.

"The museum? Are you kidding me?" replied Arlo.

To him, the museum looked terrifying. The concrete walls of the building loomed over Arlo and Isadora like an enormous evil creature. Although dim lights shined inside the building, the windows looked like black pieces of see-through metal. Sharp iron spears ran across the top of the gate like medieval booby traps intended to inflict serious harm—a visual warning to all trespassers.

"It's gorgeous," whispered Isadora, extending her hand to caress the rusty metal gate. Arlo eyed the girl, shaken by the sudden change in her demeanor. Isadora seemed to be floating, intoxicated by the brooding atmosphere.

"Sometimes darkness speaks to me like a whisper in the night. Listen. Can you hear it?"

Arlo's mouth fell open as Isadora's words oozed out into the cool night air, almost singing as she spoke.

"Y-you okay?"

"This place is filled with powerful energy. Can you feel it? It feels like someone taking hold of the very air we breathe and gently pulling it away from us."

Arlo looked at Isadora and took a slight step away from her.

"What's going on, Isadora? Why'd you bring me here?"

Isadora closed her eyes and inhaled deeply.

"Have you ever loved someone so much that you were willing to relinquish a piece of your soul?"

"A piece of my soul?"

"I've lost something, a piece of who I am, and I don't know how to get it back. I need you to help me."

"Has something happened?"

Isadora paused and took another breath.

"My parents left me."

To Arlo, the words rolled off Isadora's tongue like a secret she'd been holding inside forever.

"What do you mean?"

"They're gone. One night I came home, and they were gone."

This revelation moved Arlo, and he felt terrible for Isadora.

"That's horrible!"

Arlo looked at Isadora's face, expecting tears, but instead, he saw only an empty, emotionless shell of a girl.

"Just little old me in a big house."

"Where did they go?"

"I wish I knew."

"Did you tell the police? I mean, there are laws to stop parents from—"

Before Arlo could finish his sentence, Isadora interrupted him.

"All I have is you, my Arlo."

The emotion in Isadora's voice made Arlo uncomfortable, and he wanted to change the subject. Sure, he liked Isadora, but in light of her revealing her secret, Arlo didn't want to have so much responsibility for her happiness.

"Why are we here?" asked Arlo, looking to change the subject.

Suddenly Isadora turned to face the museum again and nodded toward the building.

"The key to getting my parents back is inside."

"Really? What's in there?"

Isadora took another deep breath.

"Okay, I know this will sound weird, but you've got to believe me. Everything I'm telling you is true."

"I'm listening."

"When my parents left me, I barely slept and stayed awake four, sometimes five days in a row. Things were intense for me, and I started hearing voices."

Arlo couldn't hide the skepticism on his face.

"Voices?"

"Yeah. I was hearing voices all the time. For a while, I thought I was going crazy. And that's when I started hearing John."

"John?"

"He told me his parents abandoned him, too, and he's been alone for ten years."

Arlo twisted his face in disbelief.

"I don't know about this, Isadora."

Isadora grabbed Arlo by his shoulders and shook him.

"Just listen to me!"

"Okay, Isadora. Calm down. I'm listening."

Isadora lowered her voice and began revealing everything to Arlo.

"As I said, I thought I was going crazy. I told myself this continuously: 'Don't listen to John, Isadora. It's your mind playing tricks on you.' I thought I was going batshit crazy—until John told me I would meet you."

"Me?"

"Can you believe it? He told me your name and everything. I remember his exact words: 'One day, you'll meet Arlo, and he'll be the one to help you find your parents.' John told me I'd meet you at school, and I did."

"You do realize this John is a figment of your imagination, don't you?"

"I don't think so. John taught me things. He gave me a taste of his power and taught me how to move things with my mind. That thing with Nathan at school? John taught me how to do that."

Arlo's mouth dropped open.

"What? Are you telling me that Nathan's injuries were real?"

Isadora was quiet for a while.

"Well?"

"I didn't hurt Nathan. I just made his mind think he was hurt."

Arlo shook his head in disbelief.

"You expect me to believe that crap? How stupid do you think I am?"

"I know it sounds crazy, but John showed me how."

"You need help, Isadora."

"I don't! John's real!"

"Stop this nonsense. John is all in your mind."

"He isn't!"

"No? Didn't you tell me we were in the same class previously? You already knew my name. This John voice was just your mind playing tricks on you."

"Well . . . about the school thing. I lied a little. We were never in the same class."

"You lied?"

"I didn't want to freak you out. How would you respond if I came up to you and said, 'Hey, I like you because some voice in my head told me to like you?' You would've run like hell away from me."

Not sure how to take Isadora's confession, Arlo remained silent.

"John told me about the room inside the museum. It's where I can find all the answers about my parents."

Arlo turned away from Isadora and started walking home.

"I'll see you in school tomorrow."

Isadora ran to Arlo and grabbed him by the arm.

"Please, Arlo! I can't do this alone!"

Arlo spun around and yanked Isadora's hand from his arm.

"You lied to me! Who knows what else you lied about?"

"Okay, you have a right to be angry. What I did was a complete dick move, and I'm sorry about that. But I didn't lie about anything else. My feelings for you are real."

"Whatever."

"Don't tell me you don't have feelings for me. I know you do. And I have them for you. It's the only part of this whole thing that I have never doubted."

The sincerity in Isadora's eyes calmed Arlo, and he relented.

"You didn't have to lie to me," he mumbled. Isadora walked up to him and put her arms around his waist.

"I know that was a fucked-up thing to do. Please forgive me."

Isadora kissed Arlo softly and followed the kiss with another gentle embrace. After a while, Arlo felt himself melt in Isadora's arms. Finally, he pulled back, smiling bashfully.

"It's cool. I'm going home now. We can talk about it tomorrow."

"So you're just going to leave me here?"

"No, we're both going home. We can come back some other night. But I'm tired now, and I'm not feeling this place."

As Arlo slowly walked away, Isadora spoke loud enough for him to hear her.

"You know what John told me?"

The question got Arlo's attention, and he stopped.

"What did he tell you?"

"I only have two days to find my parents. If I miss the opportunity, they'll be gone forever."

"Look, Isadora, we've already discussed this. The voice is your imagination playing tricks on you."

"I've been alone for months. If you were in my position, what would you do?"

"I'd go to the police."

Isadora smiled and turned away from Arlo.

"It's okay, Arlo. Go home. But I can't wait another night knowing there's a possibility of ending this nightmare. I'm going in there. And if I die alone, so be it."

"Die? What, in that museum? That's not fair. You're trying to force me to go in with you."

"You don't know what it's like to be so alone—to go home to an empty house night after night, to sit in silence waiting for the day the electricity will stop working, or thinking about where you're going to steal food. I don't know if I can take it much longer. I have to go inside tonight. I need to know where my parents are."

Isadora walked hurriedly to the gate while Arlo stood back, contemplating if he should go in. Isadora grabbed the metal gate, placed one of her feet inside the cracks, and climbed to the top. By the time she landed on the other side, Arlo was straddled atop the fence, preparing to slide down.

"You sure there's no one inside?" he asked as he slid cautiously down.

"John told me there's one guard," replied Isadora. "He's probably sleeping now."

"Great. *John* told you."

The two teens moved closer to the shadowed walls and shimmied around the side until they disappeared in the darkness.

12

For Love and the Unknown

After making their way along the side of the museum, Arlo and Isadora pushed toward the rear. As they moved beyond the shadows, Arlo felt it was safe to stroll out into the open and proceeded to boldly proceed along the lit path on the side of the building. Suddenly, Isadora grabbed his arm, yanked Arlo back into the shadows, and pointed toward the roof where two rotating cameras were recording. Isadora motioned for Arlo to follow her away from the building, and the two ducked behind a row of large bushes until they finally came out in front of two tall steel doors—the back doors of the museum.

"Geez. Why do you think the doors are so big?" asked Arlo.

"You came here for a field trip, right? Didn't you see that T-Rex in there? How else were they supposed to get that thing inside?" replied Isadora.

Arlo softly placed one of his hands on the metal door handle and pulled on it.

"It's locked. Judging from the size of these doors, they probably use a digital security system to secure the building."

Isadora pointed to two large windows positioned atop the building.

"We can't go in through the windows. They're too high up."

"Great. I guess it's time for us to go home."

Frustrated by Arlo's desire to leave, Isadora mumbled something, reached out, and pulled on one of the door handles. There was a dull clicking sound, and then both doors opened.

"How'd you do that?" asked Arlo in disbelief. "I pulled on those doors, and they were locked."

Isadora closed her eyes and spoke in a whispered voice.

"I hear you, John. I know you're here guiding me."

Arlo could do nothing but stare at his girlfriend. Although he didn't believe what Isadora told him about voices, seeing her whispering to herself was unnerving. And worse, Arlo couldn't discount what his eyes witnessed—that the locked door wasn't open when he tried it, but it magically unlocked as soon as Isadora touched the handle.

Arlo and Isadora walked through the doors and into a large room. Although the ceiling lights were out, the lighting coming from inside numerous display cases cast a mystical glow throughout the building.

"This place gives me the creeps," whispered Arlo, his voice echoing louder than he expected. Isadora didn't respond and continued moving quickly through the exhibits.

"Where are we going?" asked Arlo as they moved deeper into the building.

Isadora ignored Arlo's question and mumbled under her breath. Suddenly she stopped, rubbed her eyes, and began blinking furiously.

"What are you doing?" asked Arlo.

Isadora ignored Arlo's question and continued her conversation with the voice in her head.

"Is it here?" she whispered, pointing past the enormous triceratops exhibit. "Where? This way? Are you sure?"

Frustrated by Isadora's insistence that she was holding a conversation with her imaginary friend, Arlo angrily lashed out at his girlfriend.

"Have you lost it or something? Nobody is here except us! Stop pretending you're talking to someone in your head because it's freaking bonkers!" whispered Arlo.

"But I am. Can't you hear John's voice? He's the one that opened the door for us," replied Isadora.

Arlo shook his head in disbelief.

Suddenly Isadora grabbed Arlo's hand.

"This way!" she exclaimed, quickly pulling Arlo toward the darkened area she'd previously identified.

Arriving at the edge of the wall, the two teens slowly peered around the corner and saw a dull light coming from a separate room. Arlo and Isadora tiptoed to the room and looked inside—an overweight security guard sat in a chair in front of several monitors, sound asleep with his security hat on his face. Isadora and Arlo darted past the room and down a long corridor until they finally arrived at the entrance of another room. Isadora closed her eyes and placed her hand on the door.

"It's in here?" she asked her invisible friend. "Are you sure?"

Arlo could take no more. He stopped walking.

"Isadora, I'm going home. You're not making any—"

Suddenly the door swung open, and Arlo jumped back in surprise.

"What the hell?" he asked, terrified at what he had witnessed.

But Isadora didn't move. Instead, she peered into the dark room and continued mumbling. Finally, she grabbed Arlo's arm and pulled him along with her.

"There's no need to be afraid. John's here with us."

But Arlo *was* afraid. He felt like something was pulling him into Isadora's imaginary world. Something terrible was happening, and no matter how he tried to deny it, he felt like he was losing control of the situation. For the first time since they'd been together, Arlo was afraid of Isadora; she was placing herself in danger and pulling Arlo along with her.

As they walked to the center of the dark room, a strange odor suddenly engulfed Arlo's nose, causing him to wince.

"You smell that?"

"Shhhh."

"But something stinks. Can't you smell it?"

"It's your imagination."

Arlo pulled his T-shirt over his mouth and nose.

"My God! It smells like something died in here!"

But Isadora didn't hear him. She was in a catatonic state, seemingly gliding through the darkness toward something only she could see.

"Where is it, John?" she whispered. "Tell me."

Suddenly Arlo felt a jolt of energy course through his body, and he stopped in his tracks. Something wasn't right. He didn't know why, but he felt a fear inside that he'd never felt before. He began trembling as he nervously scanned the darkness. Something was in the room with them—a presence. The thick, pungent odor grew, allowing Arlo to identify familiar smells within its composition: his grandmother's room as she laid in bed sick, waiting on his mother to change her diaper; the burning smell of ammonia, and the metallic odor of rusting iron, which smelled oddly like the truck in his grandmother's yard. Soon Arlo also identified something within the odor that sickened his soul—the moldy scent of cemetery soil that he'd smelled at his cousin's funeral, an event he hadn't thought about in years. Arlo had been so affected by his cousin's death that he'd blocked it out. But now, the odor brought his cousin back in a tidal wave of sadness. He remembered the coldness of his cousin's face when he'd reached out to touch it during his wake.

Arlo quickly tried to clear his mind, but he couldn't. The odor was too strong. It was in the room with them, crawling over them, inside them, through them—making him remember things he didn't want to remember.

"Let's get out of here, Isadora!"

Arlo reached out for Isadora's arm, but she pulled away, whispering as she continued walking into the darkness.

"I've come just as you instructed, John. Now show me."

Arlo slowly started backpedaling to the door.

"Fuck this! I'm gone! Do you hear me, Isadora? I'm leaving!"

Suddenly the door slammed shut behind Arlo. He ran to the door and began yanking on the handles.

"What's going on?" he yelled, turning back to Isadora. "It's locked!"

Suddenly a faint white light appeared, revealing a much smaller door at the back of the room.

"What's that?" asked Arlo. Isadora raised her arms and began laughing hysterically, spinning in circles, enthralled by what was happening.

"I did it!" she yelled.

Arlo was terrified. He started pulling on the door harder, kicking it, trying to break the lock while continuously looking at the small door on the other side of the room.

"Help! Is anyone out there?" he yelled. Arlo didn't care if the security guard heard him—he wanted out.

Isadora fell to her knees and pulled out a knife.

"I brought him to you just as you requested. Now give it to me. The glory is mine!"

Isadora screamed as she ran the sharp blade across her cheek, creating a deep wound that immediately started bleeding heavily. She wiped the blood off her face and smeared it on the floor in a circle.

"As I position myself in the center of this covenant circle, let this spilled blood serve as a promise to you, John. A promise of loyalty to the power of the darkness. From this day forward, my life and body are yours to do with as you desire. Let the night consume me!"

Isadora grabbed the knife and plunged it into her thigh. She screamed in pain and fell on her side, laughing uncontrollably and writhing in delight.

"Isadora! Are you out of your mind? What the hell are you doing?"

"He's here! I can feel it!"

The light underneath the small door grew brighter and brighter, bathing the room in brilliance, temporarily blinding Arlo, and making him recoil against the exit. Soon Arlo felt the metal door burning his back. He turned around and reached out to grab one of the handles, and screamed out in agony—the door was so hot, his hand stuck to the handle. Arlo could smell his flesh burning and struggled to free himself, pulling harder as the searing pain reduced him to a crumpled mess on his knees in front of the door. Unable to tolerate the pain much longer, he gave one final pull and freed himself, tearing the top layer of skin from his palm. Arlo fell to the floor in agony, sweating profusely, clutching his blistering hand and watching Isadora on her knees facing the other door.

"Isadora!" yelled Arlo. "Help me!"

But Isadora didn't move.

"Give me what I want!" she screamed.

The light underneath the door suddenly went out, and everything was black. The only sound was Arlo's heavy breathing and whimpering as he struggled with the pain of his burned hand.

Suddenly there was an explosion, and the tiny door in the back of the room flew open. A thick, lumpy brown liquid began spraying all over the room. Arlo recoiled in horror as gobs of the fluid clung to the walls, covered the air in a foul stench, and spread filth all over the floor. He soon started gagging, realizing the liquid was the source of the stench he'd smelled. The odor swallowed him whole, and he tried holding his breath, but nothing could give him reprieve from the toxic sludge that flooded the room.

Arlo scrambled to his feet, and again reached for the door behind him.

"Let me out!" he yelled, clawing at the door with his uninjured hand.

But the liquid kept pouring into the room.

"Isadora! Do something!"

But the girl remained possessed. She moved closer to the stream of filth and howled in pleasure as the disgusting liquid covered her body.

"Take me! I am yours!" screamed Isadora while opening her mouth, attempting to consume the slimy substance.

And then it stopped.

As if something had taken away all his senses, Arlo could neither see nor hear anything. The stream of sewage filling the room, the hellish glow, and Isadora's wild behavior were all gone.

"Am I dead?" asked Arlo, his voice echoing through the darkness. Soon he heard the moaning of Isadora from the floor.

"Isadora? You there?"

"Yeah. I'm here."

"What happened?"

Arlo looked at the tiny room. Although the door was missing, a dull light shone inside, allowing Arlo to look around. The mud on the floor and walls was gone, and the whole room looked like they had never entered.

"What the hell's going on?" he asked incredulously.

Arlo raised himself from the floor and looked at his hand—it was uninjured, and there was no missing skin or blisters—only the wound from the cut he'd made earlier. Arlo gave Isadora a bewildered look. Slowly Isadora raised herself from the floor and ran her fingers along her cheek. She looked down at her thigh.

"Are you injured?" asked Arlo.

"No," Isadora replied.

Both Isadora and Arlo looked at the small room. Slowly Isadora began creeping toward it.

"Are you crazy?" asked Arlo. "Let's get out of here."

Arlo backed away from Isadora and felt for the door handle behind him. When he heard the door click, he turned to look in surprise— it was open! Arlo opened the door and prepared to make his dash. He looked again at Isadora as she inched toward the entrance to the other room.

"Last chance, Isadora. I'm leaving."

But Isadora continued moving toward the tiny room. Arlo said nothing and turned away from his girlfriend to leave. As soon as he walked through the door, a small child with black eyes stepped into his path.

"They don't love you," said the child with a deep demonic voice.

Arlo stumbled back, terrified.

"You know they don't love you. Come to us. Join us."

The child took a step closer.

"Their death is your salvation. It is the only way."

Arlo turned away from the child and froze—dozens of children now surrounded him.

"Isadora!" Arlo screamed.

The children continued staring at Arlo with black eyes, motionless and unresponsive. Some children were young, and some were teenagers, but all wore the same stench of evil, their black eyes staring through Arlo into nothingness.

"They don't love you. Your destiny is with us," the children spoke in unison.

Arlo could feel his heart. He tried calming himself but started hyperventilating as fear overcame him. He didn't understand what was happening.

Finally, his eyes fell on Isadora. Two teenage boys were holding her by her wrists. The boys scared Arlo; their faces bore unnatural smiles, their mouths almost too big for their tiny faces, fashioned in such a way as though they seemed artificially attached. One child had blond hair with clumps of dirt in it. His face wasn't soiled, but the boy still seemed filthy; his discolored skin had small brown patches around his eyes. Arlo had seen the look before; it was the look of the dying. His cousin had the same look while in the hospital, dying of cancer.

The other boy was African American with dreadlocks hanging from his head. Arlo didn't see the same circles of decay around his eyes; instead, the dark-skinned boy had a tinge of grayness to his skin, like he was dead—a walking corpse whose transition to death was complete.

Suddenly the blond-haired boy raised his hand and slapped Isadora across the face.

"Isadora!" Arlo yelled.

But she couldn't hear him. The catatonic look on her face had returned; her eyes were open, but she was unresponsive.

One teenager lifted Isadora's limp face and gently kissed her lips. The act startled Arlo more than the violent assault, and he briefly turned away. When he looked again, the filthy blond-haired boy opened his mouth, extended a long, purple, lizard-like tongue, and ran it across Isadora's hands, arms, and face.

A sickening feeling crept into the back of Arlo's throat, and he felt like vomiting. Seeing the evil teens handle his girlfriend while she remained unaware made anger boil inside Arlo's chest. He wanted to fight back, to defend Isadora, but he looked about the room and realized fighting was something he couldn't do. Undoubtedly, the other evil-looking children were with the two boys, and any attempt at aggression would trigger an attack he would not survive. Slowly, Arlo lowered his eyes in defeat and tried not to watch.

The two teens noticed Arlo's passive behavior and twisted their strange mouths into grotesque smirks; seeing Arlo struggling with the dilemma seemed to delight them. They opened their mouths and released soft whooshing sounds into the room, their way of laughing, seemingly ridiculing the boy. Their evil mockery burned at Arlo's emotions like pieces of hot coal. He hated people laughing at him, and the boys seemed to know this weakness.

Suddenly the blond teen made a fist and struck Isadora again, but this time much harder. Both boys turned to look at Arlo, hoping to see another tortuous emotional explosion. Arlo tried his best to maintain his composure but couldn't. He could feel anger boiling deep inside that he'd never felt before. He wanted to run to the boys and pummel them with his fists. Isadora didn't deserve their abuse.

Arlo began trembling with anger. He had to do something. Muting his fear and using the rage he felt to fuel his courage, Arlo clenched his fists and prepared to run at the boys.

But suddenly, Isadora began stirring. After struggling to raise her head, she blinked and looked around the room.

"Is he here?" she finally asked her captors.

Arlo unclenched his fists.

"Isadora, are you okay?" he asked, taking a step in her direction.

Bleeding from her left temple and drooling, Isadora didn't acknowledge Arlo. Instead, she looked past her captors and yelled to the small door in the back of the room.

"Where the fuck is he?" she asked. "He's supposed to be here!"

Isadora tried freeing herself from the two boys, but they held her arms tight.

"Who the hell are you guys? Why isn't he here?"

The two boys responded by twisting their distorted mouths into smirks. Ignoring the boys, Isadora yelled toward the room.

"You bastards! I've done everything he asked of me. I demand you fulfill your promise!"

Arlo's knees grew weak. He couldn't believe what he was hearing.

"Isadora! You said . . ."

Isadora turned to Arlo and exploded in anger.

"Shut up, you sniveling baby! John told me to bring you here, and I did!"

Arlo was furious.

"You lying bitch! I guess that story about your parents was a lie, too."

Isadora burst into laughter, and all the children in the room joined her.

"You're so gullible. My parents *are* missing, but they didn't abandon me; I gave them to John as a gift for the unimaginable power he will bestow upon me."

Suddenly a violent earthquake began shaking the room and threw Arlo to the ground. He quickly climbed to his feet and attempted to run, but as soon as he took one step, his whole body went limp, and he crashed to the floor. He tried to stand again, but all his energy was gone. All he could do was lie on the ground, watching the tiny entrance at the back of the room.

Suddenly Arlo felt a sickness course through his body like a burst of electricity. Dizziness overcame him, and the room started spinning. Within seconds, vomit shot from his mouth and sprayed across the floor. His stomach started cramping, and Arlo hurled again, pushing a red liquid out of his mouth that tasted like iron. Realizing it was blood, Arlo began to whimper between his struggles to catch his breath. Sharp pain moved through his stomach like thunder, making the cramps squeeze and twist his intestines into knots.

"Please! Make it stop!" Arlo yelled.

He screamed in agony as his stomach growled loudly, swelling and vibrating like something was inside. Arlo wrapped his arms around his belly and his face flushed with blood, warming his cheeks and making his eyes water. Suddenly his stomach rose and fell one final time, and a long bellow echoed throughout the room. Arlo breathed deeply and tried to hold on, but he couldn't—his bowels emptied, and a pool of blackened filth covered the floor beneath him. He began crying from embarrassment, mortified at losing control over his bodily functions.

"Look at him!" screamed Isadora. "He's fucking crying! Can you believe it?"

The children began cackling in high-pitched laughter, covering their mouths and pointing at Arlo as he wallowed in filth.

Suddenly a thick brown liquid began spraying from the room, covering everything in shit. Once more, he tried moving his legs and was thrilled to see that his appendages moved at his command.

13

John

Suddenly, the children all began repeating a name.

"JOHN. JOHN. JOHN."

As if terrified, the children's black eyes grew large like two giant dark holes in the center of their faces, revealing empty, vein-filled skulls without brains. They began shrieking in high-pitched screams and threw themselves to the floor, rubbing the brown muck all over themselves, bowing repeatedly.

"JOHN. JOHN. JOHN," they repeated.

Suddenly two gigantic claws covered in mud grabbed the edges of the small room and ripped at the walls, tearing them apart.

Isadora was in euphoria, her eyes dancing as she smiled uncontrollably.

"He's here!" she screamed, her eyes ablaze with anticipation.

Plaster and drywall flew about the room as the claws tore the wall away. Little by little, the opening grew larger until an enormous beast shoved its head into the space. The creature resembled a wolf with muddy black fur, its long claws ripping at the air as it growled and banged its head against the opening. Each time the animal placed its face in the space, it looked at Arlo and Isadora with its searing red eyes and became enraged, thrashing about and ripping at the wall more ferociously, slinging mud from its jowls. The monster curled its lips back and revealed a mouth filled with sharp, long teeth the size of a human forearm. Its howl was so terrifying that even the demonic children recoiled in terror.

Finally, the creature burst through the opening, sending the remaining pieces of plaster flying across the room. It raised its head, released another bellow, and lunged toward Isadora.

Arlo got his first look at the creature's body and almost fainted. He had never seen something so disgusting in his life. A portion of the hell-dog's body was missing, and its heart and lungs were visible. Flies and gnats buzzed around its entrails while a thick coating of plump maggots clung to its flesh, biting and laying eggs.

The odor from the creature's wounds sent a new explosion of rot and decay into the air. Arlo held his breath but didn't turn away, afraid doing so would provoke an attack by the beast. At that moment, he noticed a muddy chain attached to the monster's neck. He looked past the creature into the room and saw a towering, hooded figure cloaked in black leathery garb. Suddenly the figure yanked the chain, and the demon dog released a cry of pain. The monster immediately turned and sat obediently in front of the room, waiting for its master's entrance.

Finally, the hooded figure entered the room. It extended a long, stained human hand with grotesquely long fingernails from underneath the muddy leather garb, and reached out to pet the head of the demon dog.

"To walk amongst the soft earth of the fallen is a privilege unworthy of the weak," the children all whispered.

Isadora pushed her captives away and knelt before the hovering, hooded figure.

"It's me, John. Don't you remember me?"

The hooded figure stood unresponsive.

"I did as you asked. You see?"

Isadora pointed to Arlo as he crouched on the floor.

The figure tilted its head to look at Arlo, and the demon dog howled.

"She did not consume their flesh," the children whispered.

Isadora started to panic.

"I know, but . . . I brought my parents here to you as an offering!"

"She did not consume the flesh."

"I . . . I just couldn't do it. I don't know why."

"She did not consume the flesh."

"Wait! I'm dedicated to you, John. I'm yours! How can I prove it?"

The figure stood silent.

"Take my body! Do with it what you must! I give everything to you!"

The children spoke again.

"What you give in your moment of pain will determine your destiny," they said, repeating the phrase three times.

Isadora seemed confused.

"What? What does that mean?"

The shadowy figure beckoned the two boys, and they lifted Isadora from the ground.

"Is this it? Are you finally going to give it to me?"

Suddenly the figure grabbed the front of his leather robe and tore it away.

Arlo screamed at what he saw. What stood in front of him wasn't a man, but seemingly a combination of several. John had a face, but it was a face of three people, sectioned and cauterized with flesh onto one enormous skull. The left part of his face drooped, pulling down his left eye to expose various veins within the eyeball. The nostril of the sagging face was large and plump, while the lip held no form, and only seemed to be shredded meat. The center of John's face was much smaller than the other two and appeared to be a child. The eye was tiny and nearly perfect in shape, while the nose was barely the size of a button on a winter coat. Its mouth was perfectly round and pink. The right side of the face was a woman's; the eye was more prominent in size than the other two, and the eyelashes were long and luxurious. The nose and lips were thin, but the cheek had a hole that oozed a dark fluid. Although the faces were together on one skull, they all moved independently, each reflecting individual personalities. The male face menaced Arlo with terrifying expressions while the female grunted and growled like a wild beast. Meanwhile, the child looked innocently about the room, throttling between looks of euphoria and sadness.

John's body was a towering mountain of muscle. The neck holding up his enormous head was so muscular that he looked like he could easily swallow a human. Long spaghetti-like veins snaked through his massive arms like thick cables. His legs were bigger but equally powerful, resembling large tree trunks propping up John's mountain of evil.

But there was something more terrifying than John's grotesque physical appearance. In the center of his broad chest, Arlo saw the impression of adult human faces pushing against John's flesh, stretching his skin as if attempting to escape, each releasing a muffled sound before disappearing.

"Oh my!" exclaimed Isadora with tears in her eyes. "So beautiful!"

John walked over and stood in front of Isadora. He extended his huge hand and touched her face. The grimacing part of John's face spoke:

"Tear her apart!"

And then the female part:

"Her screams will be so deliciously sinister."

And finally, the child:

"I see love in her eyes."

John extended his index finger and touched the center of Isadora's forehead. Excited, Isadora began smiling and clapping her hands.

"It's here! Finally! Thank you so much, John. You don't know how long I've waited for this moment. Now I'll finally be able to . . . AAAAAHHHH!!!"

Suddenly Isadora's arms jerked back, breaking her shoulders and sending a loud crunching sound throughout the room. As she levitated, Isadora broke into a hysterical laugh.

"I can take the pain! HAHAHAHAHA . . . I can take it, John! I can do this!"

John said nothing. Instead, he calmly grabbed the helldog's chain and pulled it closer to Isadora, all three faces smiling as an invisible force crushed the girl's bones. Arlo could do nothing but watch as Isadora's legs broke like twigs, each broken bone sounding like a loud firecracker.

Isadora began sweating profusely, and John moved even closer. He grabbed Isadora's broken arm and lifted it, pulling her fingers close to his chest. As soon as he did, two faces appeared in his flesh, moaning and crying as they took turns trying to escape.

"Isadora!"

"Free us!"

"We love you!"

"It hurts so much!"

Isadora was both crying and laughing.

"Mommy? Daddy? Is that you?"

"Isadora! Please!"

"Why did you do this to us?"

Isadora's face hardened, and she took the pain without grimacing.

"You did this! You! Daddy did things to me, and I told you about it, Mommy! I told you! And what did you do? Nothing! You just continued sewing or whatever stupid shit you were doing! Fuck you! I hope you rot in hell!"

Suddenly John's child face opened his mouth wide and released a terrifying cry.

"Waaaaaaaahhhhh!"

Arlo covered his ears and trembled anew. He could tell the baby's cries signified that something horrible was coming.

John pulled the dog closer to Isadora.

"Do it!" yelled John's evil face, his mouth drooling with thick brown mud as its eye widened. *"I want to see it! Do it now!"*

"It is time for the cries of the wicked," joined the female face, mud leaking from her mouth.

"Waaaaaaahhh," cried the child's face. Suddenly blood began pouring from its eye.

John extended a long finger and pushed Isadora in the center of her forehead. A loud snap sounded throughout the room, and Isadora went limp from the waist up. She tumbled back while her legs remained standing, frozen in place. Soon her eyes met Arlo's.

"You see, Arlo? This isn't so bad," she said deliriously. "This is nothing compared to the power John's going to give me.

Suddenly John yanked on the evil dog's chain and pulled it closer. He made a fist and crashed it into the devil dog's spine, causing the monster to release a whimper, open its mouth, and move closer to Isadora's bent side. John struck the dog again, and it opened its mouth and clamped down on Isabela's exposed flesh. It hungrily pulled a chunk of meat, spraying Isadora's blood and body fluids throughout the room. The beast gorged on Isadora's flesh and swallowed it, leaving a vast hole inside the body.

"AAAAAHHHHH!" screamed Isadora, reaching out for Arlo. She began choking, and blood poured from her mouth. Arlo could do nothing except watch as his girlfriend bled uncontrollably. As though she sensed his anguish, Isadora smiled and comforted Arlo.

"It's . . .part of the process. Soon we'll be together. Wait, you'll see," Isadora whispered. She gave one last gasp and suddenly lost consciousness, her eyes open, a terrifying smile on her face.

Arlo couldn't hide his fears or his sadness. His shivering became full-blown convulsions, and his tears became thick sobs of sorrow. He knew Isadora lied to him, and maybe he was upset, yet she didn't deserve this pain. Arlo remembered the secret Isadora revealed to her mother and father, and he cried harder. All Isadora wanted was a good life; instead, her life got ruined by the people who swore to love and protect her.

Arlo looked down at Isadora's bloody face and cried harder. The irises of Isadora's eyes were white with death now, all life extinguished. Arlo felt fury inside, and he started grinding his teeth. Arlo thought of death and what would happen when the dark hour came for him. Would John come to him to take what his mother and father had given in love? Would Arlo's exit be wrapped in a blanket of pain like Isadora's, disguised as a lie?

Arlo's thoughts became darker. He started seeing the faces of the bullies that tormented him in school and felt contempt for their existence. He became lost in his mind, fantasizing about the look on the boys' faces as John tortured them, one by one, twisting their flesh until each of them apologized.

But then an image of Isadora popped into his head, and Arlo quickly returned to reality. He watched as John closed his eyes and placed his large palm on Isadora's lifeless body. All the children in the room closed their eyes, lowered themselves to the floor, and began chanting.

"She-mek-oskali! She-mek-oskali!"

John opened his three mouths and revealed white worms with metal teeth. The aggressive creatures bit and pulled at John's faces until they freed themselves, falling onto Isadora's body and entering the gaping hole in her side.

"She did not consume the flesh! She is not worthy!" yelled one face.

"Do not give her the power! She does not deserve it!" snapped the other.

"She has paid the toll. Let her join the army of the night," said the child.

Suddenly all three faces smiled.

"We agree!"

"Let her run through the darkness in search of new souls!"

"Forgo her request for power. Let her find new souls for us!"

John lowered his head and started chanting.

"Our army is growing," all three faces whispered.

Arlo saw his opportunity and bolted for the door.

14

Running From Dreams

Arlo ran through the dark museum as quickly as he could. Drenched in mud and waste, he slid and fell continuously before finally gaining footing on the marble floors. He kept looking back, expecting the demonic children to come after him at any moment. But fear propelled Arlo like a guided missile, pushing him to escape from the pit of hell without detection. As he ran past the exhibits, Arlo ignored the enormous stuffed animals and concentrated on his flight; the stuffed animals usually frightened Arlo, but after seeing actual hell in the room behind him, the dead animals posed no threat—they were toys. Arlo knew the real fear was only moments behind and would be pursuing him when they discovered he was gone.

Arlo held his breath periodically and listened—were they approaching from behind? What was the noise in the far corner of the room? Arlo called upon the acuteness of his senses to be better than ever before. He knew John's helldog would be loud, but he wasn't sure about the others; they were ghostly, like a sheet of frost appearing out of nowhere on a window.

The darkness was the hardest part. With all the tiny lights gone, everything was pitch black, making it difficult to remember things. Arlo turned a corner and got confused about his location, so he quickly turned another corner. Arlo wanted to stop and hide when he didn't recognize where he was on the third try—fearing the creatures would accost him in the dark. But then Isadora's twisted, deformed face rushed into his mind's eye, and Arlo found the strength to continue searching for his freedom.

Finally, Arlo arrived at the dinosaur exhibits.

"Almost out of here," he whispered as he pressed farther through the darkness. Arlo made a turn and came upon the security guard's room. Slowly he peered inside and saw that the security guard was still fast asleep with his hat on his face.

"Excuse me," Arlo said softly.

The officer didn't budge and remained fast asleep in the same position. Arlo moved closer and touched the officer's shoulder.

"Sir? My name's Arlo, and I need help. Can you please call the police?"

Still, the officer didn't move.

Arlo reached out and touched the guard on the shoulder. Fearing time was running out, he shook the officer more forcefully, knocking his hat off his head.

"Shit!" exclaimed Arlo.

The top of the security guard's head was missing, and hundreds of larvae were inside his skull, eating the pink brain matter and burrowing deep into his chubby neck. Arlo hadn't noticed that death had stolen upon the man earlier because of the foul odors attached to Arlo's body. But as he watched the small worms chewing on the man's brain, the smell of decomposition filled Arlo's lungs with death.

Arlo covered his mouth and backed away. Fearing that one of John's demons was in the room with him, he surveyed the room cautiously before finally turning away and breaking into a renewed sprint. Death was everywhere in the museum, and Arlo had to get out.

Searching through the darkness, Arlo spotted a familiar set of doors and ran through them. He finally made it to the massive doors at the entrance.

"Great," he said, remembering the problem he'd had trying to open them. Realizing that Isadora was no longer here to assist him, Arlo took a deep breath and pushed.

15

Friends and Enemies

When the doors opened, Arlo moved into the shadows. He couldn't believe the doors opened for him without effort and immediately suspected someone or something had unlocked the door. Arlo stood by the entrance, looking between the cracks of the door, expecting to see something jump out. When nothing did, he readied himself for a frantic dash out of the building and into the adjacent bushes. He sprinted out of the museum, immediately ran into someone, and fell.

"Arlo! What the heck, dude?"

Arlo rolled over and looked at the person on the ground beside him. It was Manuel.

"Manuel?"

"Yeah, dude. It's me," he replied, rubbing his head. "I followed you and Isadora. Where is she? Inside?"

Arlo climbed to his feet and looked back nervously into the dark building. He grabbed his friend by the arm and pulled him away from the building.

"Come on! We've got to get out of here!"

"Why? What's going on?"

"Look, it's a long story. I'll fill you in on the way home. Right now, we've got to get out of here."

Manuel paused and covered his nose.

"Dude. Did you take a dump on yourself? You stink! What's that stuff all over your clothes?"

"It's a long story. Look, let's get out of here before—"

Suddenly a loud shriek sounded from within the museum.

"What the hell was that?"

Arlo let go of Manuel's arm, and was about to take off running into the treeline when Manuel stopped him.

"Wait! I rode here on my electric scooter."

"Where'd you park it?"

"At the front gate."

Both boys sprinted around the building, jumped onto the metal fence, and began climbing. As soon as they reached the top of the gate, the two evil teenage boys Arlo saw in the room appeared at the corner of the building.

"Noooooo!" one of them screamed. Both teens' eyes burst into red flame, and they sprinted toward Arlo and Manuel.

"Dude! Who the hell are those guys?"

"Just move it!"

"But their eyes! Did you see that?"

"Let's get out of here!"

As soon as Arlo and Manuel landed on the ground, dozens of children came pouring from around the building, their eyes ablaze, shrieking and growling at the boys. Manuel jumped onto his motor scooter, and Arlo climbed on the back.

"Floor it!"

"I don't understand what's going on!"

"Just go!"

The boys took off speeding down the street with an army of possessed children chasing them. Manuel turned a corner and pulled onto another road. As soon as he did, he saw the two evil boys standing a few feet ahead in their path.

"Shit!" Manuel yelled before veering onto the sidewalk. Arlo looked behind them and saw the hoard of demonic children chasing them.

Although they had a head start on Manuel's scooter, the zombie kids were directly behind them—as though they had only moved a few feet.

"Shit, Manuel! I said floor it!"

"I did! What are these things? What the hell are you into?"

Manuel turned onto another street, and suddenly the two boys appeared again in his path, grabbing onto Arlo's shirt. Manuel turned once more and went in another direction.

"That was close, Manuel! Are you going to drive this piece of shit or what? Do something!"

"I have an idea. Hold on!"

Manuel made another sharp left and turned onto another street. He accelerated, and again the two boys appeared in his path. But this time, Manuel didn't turn away or slow down. Instead, he gripped the handlebars tightly and braced his legs for impact. The scooter slammed into the boy closest to them and drove awkwardly over his body. The other boy reached out and grabbed Arlo's leg, but Arlo delivered a perfectly timed blow to the side of his head, sending him crashing to the ground.

"Now floor it!" yelled Arlo.

Manuel accelerated and steadied the moped while Arlo quickly peered over Manuel's shoulder to see if the two boys appeared again—they didn't.

"It's working!" yelled Arlo.

"Do you mind telling me what the hell's going on?" asked Manuel.

Arlo looked back again and noticed that the children were farther away.

"They're zombies."

"Get out of here! Are you serious?"

"Yeah. But there's something much worse back there."

"What?"

"Isadora and I were in this room and—"

Before Arlo could finish his sentence, an enormous roar rose from behind them. Arlo turned to see the children falling over one another, scattering to escape.

"What's happening?" yelled Manuel.

"I don't know! I don't know!" responded Arlo.

But Arlo did know. He'd seen the gigantic snarling beast in the room on the end of a large, rusty chain; it was John's dog from hell, released by its owner to catch Arlo before he could escape.

The thunderous bellow sounded again, and Arlo turned around to see a much smaller group of children running toward him, terrified. Suddenly a large set of claws appeared out of the darkness and grabbed one of the kids, pulling him into the night. Seconds later, the monster appeared, covered in mud and snarling, tossing its head back and forth in a rage.

"Holy shit!" yelled Manuel. "What the hell is that?"

But Arlo was too afraid to respond. He watched in astonishment as the creature killed child after child without reason. A colossal paw with sharp nails stabbed one of the children in the chest and yanked him back, spraying blood across the road. The other children screamed and tried running away, but the enormous beast was too quick and powerful. Within a second, it bit into another child, ripping his body in two before the devil dog tossed back its huge head and swallowed the boy's legs. The creature immediately hunted down the boy's torso, snatched it up in its enormous mouth, and ate it. After releasing another howl, the monster smashed its head into a few fleeing children before finally giving chase to another child, eventually catching her and decapitating the girl before slashing another boy with its enormous talons.

"Manuel!" yelled Arlo. "Get us the hell out of here!"

Finally, the monster's eyes locked on Arlo and Manuel. The beast's red eyes widened, and it snarled, snapping its jaws together like two enormous vices filled with knives, slinging muddy saliva into the air. It leapt on the backs of the children and sailed through the air, almost landing on Arlo and Manuel.

"Turn, Manuel!" yelled Arlo.

"I'm trying! Shut up!" replied Manuel before turning onto a side street. Arlo looked ahead and saw a group of double-parked trucks cluttering the street.

"There! Aim for those trucks!"

Manuel sped to the semis and drove between the two closest ones. Just as he did, the monster dog crashed into the trucks and became stuck. Furious, the creature bit into the trucks, ripping at the trailers as it tried to free itself. By the time the monster broke away from the metal trap, Arlo and Manuel were gone.

16

Home

When the scooter pulled up to Manuel's house, Manuel paused for a moment.

"Go to the backyard and wait for me. I'll be out with some soap and towels."

Terrified that the monster might see them, Arlo darted into the bushes and moved stealthily to the rear of Manuel's house. After a few seconds, Manuel walked out the backdoor with two towels in hand. He quickly disrobed, went to the water faucet, turned on the hose, and pulled it into the bushes.

"Dude, we both stink. My parents will raise hell in the morning when they get a whiff of the house. Did you shit on yourself?"

Arlo didn't respond. Instead, he grabbed a bar of soap and began spraying himself with the hose. The water was ice-cold, but Arlo didn't make a sound. His whole body was numb from what he'd witnessed. After Arlo finished cleaning himself, his friend grabbed the hose and did the same. After continuously lathering himself with the soap bar, Manuel rinsed off and dried himself. He returned to Arlo and stared at him for a few moments.

"Are you going to crash here tonight?"

"I was thinking about it."

"It's probably a good idea to avoid your house tonight. Those things probably know where you live."

"Yeah."

Manuel ran his hand across his bare chest and neck, and sniffed.

"Shit! It's still on me!"

Arlo smelled his hands. The stench of the filth was still on him, like he'd never taken a bath.

"Me, too," whispered Arlo. "You got any more soap in the house?"

"Yeah. I'll get a couple more bars. We'll probably be out here for a while trying to get that smell out. I'll be back."

Manuel once again walked to his house and disappeared inside. When he emerged, he was holding a small container of bleach, two bars of soap, a bottle of his father's aftershave, and two sets of clean clothes.

"This is probably overkill, but we only have a few hours before my parents wake up. This bleach should kill most of it but be careful. Getting this stuff in your eyes or your ding-a-ling is an instant trip to the hospital. I brought a bottle of my dad's aftershave to hide any of the remaining odor. He's growing a beard now, so he'll never miss the stuff."

Manuel resprayed himself with the hose and poured a handful of bleach into his palm before rubbing it on his body. When he finished, he attacked himself once more with the bar of soap.

"So . . . are you going to tell me what happened or not?"

Arlo sprayed himself in the face with the hose, and began explaining how the most horrifying day of his life came to be. First, he told the story between grunts and grimaces as he struggled to ignore the cold water. But as he recounted what happened, he forgot the frigid water, and his body became hot—warmed by the embarrassment of falling for a girl who used him, and terrified of the existence of an evil world moving just beneath the surface of the reality he'd known.

Besides mumbling supportive words like "bitch" and "what an ass-hole," Arlo noticed Manuel didn't blame him for his bad decisions when he spoke of Isadora's betrayal. Instead, his friend listened quietly and kept his opinions to himself. When Arlo finished recounting what happened, both boys were fully dressed and smelled like they dove into a river of bleach and aftershave.

"Let me get a bag for those clothes," said Manuel as he ran into the house. When he returned, he walked to the edge of the yard, retrieved a stick, and lifted the filthy clothes into the bag.

"What am I going to do, Manuel? I'm sure that thing knows where I live."

"That's true. That skank Isadora probably told him everything about you."

"Where am I going to go? I can't stay at your house forever. What about my parents? If I tell them what happened, they'll never believe me."

"Well . . . the best thing we can do for now is to get a few hours of sleep. Neither of us can think if we don't get some rest. Come on in and crash. You can go home tomorrow morning."

Arlo sighed and shook his head in agreement. He didn't realize it before, but he was exhausted, and his body was aching. He looked around the yard to be sure nothing had followed them. Finally, Manuel and Arlo walked into the house.

17

From the Shadows

As Arlo slept, he began hearing something strange—a *thump-thump* sound vibrating from the depths of his subconscious. He ignored the noise at first because the interruption blended in with the sounds of his sleeping. But after a while, the sound grew louder.

Thump-thump.

Thump-thump.

As the sound increased, the bed began to shake with each pounding, gently and then noticeably stronger, making the bed quiver like a glass of water on a shaken table. The pounding mimicked Arlo's heartbeat, periodically beating off rhythm, making Arlo think something was wrong with his heart. Arlo began mumbling in his sleep as the sound continued.

"What's that?" he asked in his sleep. "Mom? Dad? Can you make it stop?"

Thump-thump. THUMP!

Arlo knew he was sleeping but felt like he was awake. It wasn't an unfamiliar place for him to be. He'd felt the sensation of being 'sleep-awake' before when he'd previously dreamed of winning the lottery. Realizing he didn't win, Arlo remembered trying to force himself back into the dream by searching for a quiet place in slumber. And so, he attempted to ignore the noises and tried to find a calm place that gave his body rest.

But he couldn't get to that place. The noise was too aggravating. So instead of trying to find his peaceful sleep, Arlo started listening to the noises, hoping to ride the sounds into the initiation of another dream. As he listened and concentrated, Arlo realized the sounds weren't thumps but an enormous chorus of people—whispering. Children and adults were whispering in unison from the darkness in his dreams. In time the whispers became louder, crawling out from behind the sound of Arlo's nervous heartbeat to reveal the scary whispering without cover. Still, he could only partially hear, feel, and fear the whispers—but not see the owners of those voices.

Arlo began panicking. Why couldn't he see the people? Who were they, and why had they chosen his dreams to infiltrate?

Now, something inside Arlo's sleep made him say the name.

"John."

Suddenly Arlo found himself lost within the darkness of his mind, not knowing where he was, yet searching desperately for familiarities to lead him back to a night of normal sleep. But his curiosity got the best of him, and it wasn't long before he began searching for memories of what had happened to him earlier that day. He didn't want to repeat the monster's name, but Arlo knew who was behind his nightmare—it was John, using his powers to turn Arlo's sleep against him. The whispering voices were a sneaky, ominous weapon—a warning of what potentially lay ahead and a dreadful example of John's trickery.

Although he could not see the people, something inside Arlo told him that these were the voices of the people John murdered; briefly, Arlo imagined hundreds of corpses with rotting flesh, all reaching out to Arlo from the darkness. But his mind's eye was too powerful, and Arlo quickly suppressed his imagination before he lost control. Still, as he listened, he couldn't help but wonder who these people were. Were they warning Arlo or threatening him? Arlo didn't know. The only thing he was sure of was that John had stolen their lives.

Suddenly a biting chill climbed into the bed and wrapped itself around Arlo's body. Arlo began trembling violently, his teeth chattering uncontrollably as his nose started running. Arlo's fear intensified. Soon the purpose of the voices became apparent, and Arlo began thrashing back and forth.

"They're not here to help me!" he yelled between clenched teeth. "They want to take me!"

He could feel John's victims drawing closer, collectively reaching out to drag him into a sightless hell. Arlo began choking and gasping for air.

"I can smell it," he said, trying to catch his breath. The stench of the museum coated his mouth and throat like soot. John wanted Arlo in his hell, drowning in black sludge and suffering through eternity—in his world of filth, buried underground in a place devoid of the warmth of life and love, where the sun was eternally dead and lost souls cried out in vain.

Unconsciously, Arlo grabbed the blanket, pulled it over his mouth, and began trembling as his lips turned blue. He started blowing warm breaths into the comforter, trying warm himself, but the whispering grew louder, and the room got colder. Arlo's hands and feet became ice-cold and began to ache. The whispers continued whipping through Arlo's sleep like a tattered flag blowing in the gust of a storm. Arlo could hear the whispering clearly, yet not enough to make out what the people were saying.

Suddenly the voice of a girl rang out.

"WE FOUND YOU!"

Arlo opened his eyes wide and stared up into the darkness. He recognized the voice.

"Isadora, is that you?"

The female giggled in response.

"Isadora?"

Suddenly all the voices burst into a loud tidal wave of laughter. Unable to see anyone, Arlo pulled the blanket over his head and began sobbing.

"Go away. Please, leave me alone."

But the laughter grew louder, echoing in Arlo's head like a metal spoon rattling against a giant steel drum.

"Please make it stop!" screamed Arlo.

Suddenly Arlo became filled with uncontrollable anger and lashed out at the zombies' laughter.

"I said, leave me the fuck alone!" he barked aggressively.

Suddenly something yanked the blanket off Arlo.

"STOP!"

Manuel stood in front of Arlo with a puzzled look on his face.

"Dude. What are you doing?"

Arlo opened his eyes and looked around. It was daylight, and the sun poured in through the window. Slowly Arlo raised himself on the bed. After rubbing his eyes, he zeroed in on his best friend.

"What . . . What's going on?"

"How many times do I have to wake you? Mom tried to wake you, and I've come here three times. Get up!"

"Huh? I don't remember . . ."

Arlo could still hear the whispers of the ghosts in his head. He shook his head a couple of times and rubbed his eyes.

"What time is it?"

"It's almost ten."

"Ten?! Mom's going to kill me!"

Arlo leapt from the bed and headed for the door.

"Wait!" yelled Manuel.

Arlo barely heard his friend, and paused just outside the bedroom door.

"What is it? I've got to get home."

"Dude, are you okay?"

"I'm fine. Why?"

Manuel walked over to his computer and sat down.

"Did last night happen?" asked Manuel, opening his laptop. Arlo walked back into the room and stood in front of his friend.

"It had to, right? I mean, how could we both have the same dream?"

"It's just that . . . That smell. I can't stop smelling it. My mom and dad didn't say anything about it, so I assume they can't smell it. But I can."

Annoyed, Arlo moved toward the door again.

"Look, Manuel. I've got to get home."

"You don't need to rush. My mom already called your mom and told her where you were."

Arlo relaxed a little. With Manuel's mom running interference, hopefully his parents wouldn't be too angry. Manuel's and Arlo's eyes met, and they both immediately looked elsewhere.

"Arlo."

"Yeah?"

"Something's wrong."

"No shit."

"No. I mean with me."

Arlo looked at Manuel and immediately saw the terrified look in his eyes.

"You've heard the whispers?"

"Well . . ."

"I heard them when I slept."

"Me, too. What are we going to do, Arlo? Whatever you saw in that museum is following me now."

"Let's talk after I get home. I'll give you a call in a few hours."

"Not possible. Mom is making me go to school today."

Arlo looked at his watch.

"But it's almost lunch!"

"They don't care. Mom and Dad can be assholes about school. Anyway, I'll give you a call when I get home."

"Cool."

Once again, Arlo headed for the door. Manuel stuck his head out of the bedroom as he was about to run down the stairs.

"Arlo!"

Arlo paused on the stairs and turned around.

"Yeah?"

"Whatever you do, don't tell anyone."

"You, either."

18

The Consequences of Fear

"Explain to me why you think it's okay to hang out at all times of the night without telling us?"

Arlo stood in front of his mother, tears filling his eyes. He wanted to tell her the truth, but he was too afraid. The nightmare was still fresh in his mind, tugging at the edges of reality. Although his mother hadn't spoken of the odor, Arlo could still smell the stench of mud and feces. He could feel it and taste it. Arlo quickly looked down at his shoes, expecting to see his ankles buried in thick, black sludge—but there was nothing.

"Answer me, Arlo! Now!"

Suddenly the thumping sound reappeared in Arlo's head. He tried telling himself that the sound was only his heart beating. Arlo ignored the sound and opened his mouth to speak to his mom.

"I . . . I went to Manuel's because . . ."

Arlo choked and swallowed. He couldn't finish the sentence. He tried, but nothing came out. Arlo wanted to respond to his mother, but something restrained him. Suddenly Arlo began hearing the whispering in his head—the voices were becoming louder.

"No," Arlo whispered under his breath.

"What did you say?" asked Claire, becoming angrier. "You'd better answer me this minute, young man!"

But Arlo couldn't respond because his imagination was taking over. Suddenly a burst of laughter rushed out of his mind and blared into his ears. Arlo saw his mother's lips moving, but he couldn't hear her words. The laughter filled Arlo's ears.

And then, just as quickly as the laughter began—it stopped.

Arlo waited a moment, expecting the laughter to continue, but it didn't. It was as if the voices in his head were never there. Arlo took the opportunity to respond to his mother.

"I . . . I don't think it's okay, Mom. It's just that Manuel and I forgot to—"

"You've never done something like this before, Arlo. Why now? Is it that girl?"

Arlo wished it were that simple. Still, he ignored the urge to tell his mother the truth.

"I'm sorry, Mom. It won't happen again."

Claire ignored him.

"It *is* that girl. I knew this would happen. It was only a matter of time."

"But it's not Isadora, Mom."

"No worries. I know exactly how to handle this situation. You either tell me the truth about what happened last night, or I'll ground you for so long you'll be forty the next time you leave this house."

Suddenly Isadora's voice yelled in Arlo's head.

Go ahead! Tell her! We want her to know! Tell her about John!

Isadora's voice startled Arlo, and he began nervously looking around the room.

"Do you hear me, Arlo?" asked Claire, cupping his chin and turning his head to her.

But Arlo couldn't pay attention. Isadora's voice sounded like she was in the room with them.

She doesn't love you. We know. Look at her! She can barely hide her disgust. Your presence sickens her. She speaks to your father at night, and I hear their secrets. Soon they'll come for you in the shadows.

Arlo looked down at his shoes while his mother stared at him, searching for truth in his body language. Suddenly Arlo heard Isadora's voice again:

Go ahead and rat me out.

John takes care of me now.

Just another stupid boy pretending to be something he's not.

"Well? I know you saw her last night!"

"No, Mom. Well, not exactly."

"Not exactly? What does that mean?"

Arlo stopped talking. He'd told his mother more than he should've.

"So, you're going to lie to me, now? Is that it?"

Still, Arlo remained silent.

"Fine. You're grounded."

Arlo immediately protested.

"Wait! That's not fair! I was just down the street with Manuel."

"You're grounded!"

"But, Mom . . . you don't understand."

Claire crossed her arms and turned away.

"No video games, no visiting Manuel, and no telephone or TV for two weeks."

"But I have to speak to Manuel! You don't understand! Something . . ."

Arlo caught himself before finishing his sentence, and Claire noticed.

"What? Let's hear it! Go ahead and tell me another lie, why don't you?"

Arlo turned away and began walking to his room. Just as he began climbing the stairs, Claire yelled after him.

"Just wait until your father gets home!"

Arlo slammed the door and threw himself on the bed. After a few seconds, he jumped off the bed and opened the door. Although Isadora's voice was silent, he didn't want to be alone in his room because his imagination was playing tricks on him.

A few seconds later, he heard his mom stomping up the stairs. Claire walked into his room and held out her hand.

"Unplug that phone and give it to me."

Arlo sighed and did as his mother instructed. Claire snatched the phone from his hand, walked to the TV, and unplugged it.

"I meant what I said. You're grounded!"

Claire stormed out of the room and slammed the door behind her. Once again, Arlo got up and opened the door. No matter what his mom said, there was no way he'd be staying inside. It was only a matter of time before John appeared at his house. He had to meet with Manuel to devise a plan to defend his family.

19

A Family's Love

Arlo spent the rest of the day in his room. Unlike Manuel's parents, Arlo's mom didn't pressure him to return to class. Instead, she kept a watchful eye on him to be sure he didn't break his punishment.

Arlo didn't mind. He hadn't planned on staying inside, but after thinking more about the situation, he decided he wanted to stay close to home; John's servants were out there searching for him. Staying in his room wasn't perfect, but at least he'd be safe, far away from the terrible world he'd witnessed.

He opened the blinds and allowed the sunlight to pour into his bedroom. He didn't know why but the sun pushed the horrible memories of the museum out of his mind. Arlo's mother walked past his bedroom several times to be sure he was adhering to his punishment, but Arlo could tell she was remorseful about their conversation. She could never hold an angry posture against him for longer than an hour, nor could he against her. Arlo loved his mother, and despite their problems, he felt bad about keeping her in the dark.

When Arlo's father came home, he didn't bother dropping his briefcase. Instead, he walked directly to Arlo's room.

"Hey, Dad."

Jaime sighed and placed his briefcase on the floor.

"What is this about?"

"Nothing, Dad. I just wanted to talk to Manuel about some stuff, and I lost track of time."

Jaime cracked a smile, walked to the bed, and sat down.

"This is about that girl?"

"No. Well, not really."

"Look. We've all been there before. The first girlfriend is always special and can make your mind do strange things."

Arlo looked away.

"How's that?"

"Look. You can run that *I don't know* game on your mom, but not on me."

"It's not a game. I just . . ."

"Look. I'm not going to ask you anything embarrassing. You need to understand that there are rules, and you need to follow them. Sneaking out at night is not the smartest thing you've done. You could've been hurt, or worse."

"Sorry, Pop."

"You know how your mom gets. Ease up, okay?"

Jaime stood and headed to the door.

"There has to be some kind of punishment."

"I know. Mom grounded me for two weeks."

Jaime seemed surprised.

"Two weeks?! Jeez! She doesn't play!"

Arlo smiled.

"I know, right?"

"I'll see if she'll make your punishment a little shorter, but it's her decision."

Arlo smiled.

"Thanks, Dad!"

"A new girlfriend is always difficult for mothers, and you're her only child. Try to move softly."

Jaime chuckled.

"Isadora's got your nose open, huh?"

"No, Dad. It's not like that."

"You and I need to have that talk soon."

"What talk?"

"You know, the birds and the bees."

Arlo blushed.

"Aw, Dad. Stop it."

"Straighten up. Dinner's almost ready."

Jaime lightened the mood at dinner by telling everyone of a hilarious event that happened to him at work. Right before entering a meeting, he went to wash his hands in the bathroom, and the faucet sprayed water all over the front of his pants, making it appear as if he'd had an accident. Claire laughed so hard that water gushed out of her nose. Arlo couldn't contain himself, and all three of them giggled through dessert. By the time Arlo cleared the table, Claire had rescinded his punishment and made him promise not to repeat the infraction.

After showering and watching a little TV, Arlo retrieved his phone from his mother. He plugged it in and dialed most of Manuel's number, but Arlo paused before he dialed the last digit. Did he want to discuss the previous night's events before bed? Doing so would trigger terrifying thoughts that would keep him awake. Slowly, Arlo hung up the phone.

"I'll talk to him later," he whispered.

Before climbing into bed, Arlo walked over to the window and peered outside. Aside from a stray cat strolling across the yard, nothing seemed out of the ordinary. The security lights from the house lit up the backyard just as they had hundreds of times before.

Arlo yawned and stretched. At that moment, he realized he was exhausted. So much had happened; all he wanted was a good night's sleep. Opening his bedroom door and turning out the light, Arlo climbed into bed and closed his eyes. Within a few seconds, he was fast asleep.

20

The Night Son

Arlo woke up suddenly and sat upright in bed. Something wasn't right. Everything was dark, and there was no light showing from the hallway. Arlo rubbed his eyes and looked more closely; his bedroom door was closed. He tried not to panic.

Mom probably closed it before she went to bed, Arlo thought.

There was nothing strange about his mother closing his bedroom door before retiring because she wanted Arlo to have his privacy.

But as much as Arlo tried pretending nothing was out of the ordinary, he could feel that something was different. The house had an unfamiliar feeling, like he was a stranger trespassing in a place he didn't belong. His bedroom didn't feel like it was his. Although the room was barely big enough to hold a bed and dresser, it now felt as large as an empty gymnasium, too big for Arlo.

Arlo pulled the blankets up to his nose and sniffed. The sheets were clean, and the fragrance of his mother's favorite detergent was there, just as it always had been.

But . . .

The fragrance on the sheets made Arlo feel sick—disgusted, even. His stomach bubbled, and a feeling of nausea overcame him. Now the sheets seemed *too* clean. Disgustingly so. Arlo pulled at the sheets until he grabbed the portion closest to the floor. He longed for a bit of filth, grime, and dust—anything to take away his awful feeling. His mother's clean sheets made Arlo want to vomit.

"I can't take this," Arlo snapped.

He jumped up from the bed and stripped away the blankets. He had to get rid of the blankets before he vomited all over the room. He walked over to the window and prepared to toss the sheets onto the lawn when a buzzing noise sounded. Arlo dropped the blankets on the floor. After a few seconds, he heard the buzzing gain.

"What is that?" he whispered, fearing the worst.

Arlo moved closer to the center window. It seemed different than all the others. He couldn't see through the glass because it seemed almost liquid, made of shiny, translucent material. Arlo stuck out his index finger to touch the window. Suddenly the material he'd thought was glass moved away from his finger. There was a buzz near his ear. Then aagain. And again. Arlo reached out and planted his palm on the window.

"Flies!" he whispered.

Arlo slammed his palm against the window, squashing a mound of insects before picking them up in his fist. Suddenly, buzzing flies filled the air around him. Arlo should've been disgusted, but he wasn't. Arlo felt a calm wash over him as the files struck his face and buzzed in his ears. Without thinking, he shoved the fistful of dead flies into his mouth. The taste was bitter and metallic, reminding Arlo of the time Manuel dared him to put dirty pennies in his mouth.

Calmly, he moved his tongue around, allowing the bugs to drown in his saliva. Arlo could tell some of the insects were still alive, twitching between his teeth and tickling his throat, yet he swallowed the bugs and smiled; he had never realized that eating the insects would be so delicious. Sucking the last fly corpse out of his teeth, Arlo went to the window and began searching for more of the insects. But he only found insect ooze remaining on the glass. Disappointed, and with a hunger to eat more of the bugs gnawing at his stomach, Arlo ran his tongue all over the window, slurping the bug guts. When Arlo finished, he began swatting at the air, trying to catch more flies in his hands.

"Please . . . I've got to have some more!" he said desperately, thick saliva dripping from his mouth.

But the insects were gone.

Arlo paused in the middle of the floor to think about what had just happened. Soon he began gagging, heaving at what he'd just done.

"I ate flies!" he yelled incredulously, wiping his tongue.

Suddenly Arlo burst into tears.

"I don't understand what's happening to me."

But deep inside, Arlo knew what was happening—it was John.

Arlo stood, wiped the tears away, and walked back to the window. He yanked open the blinds and froze. Standing on the lawn were the two teenage boys that had pursued him at the museum. They wore white robes, each carrying a small wooden box underneath their arm. Their eyes glowed an eerie green, making them even more frightening.

"Shit!" whispered Arlo before ducking down to hide. Both boys looked up at the same time as if they heard him. Arlo got down on both knees and crawled to his bedroom door. He had to get his mother and father out of the house. As Arlo inched open the door, a familiar putrid odor engulfed his lungs, making him cough uncontrollably. A damp sweat began dripping down Arlo's back, and he started trembling in fear—the boys were in the house.

"I've got to get to Mom and Dad," he whispered, trying to control his fear. He crawled out into the hallway, and was about to descend the stairs when he saw the two boys at the bottom—their glowing eyes staring directly at him.

"Shit!" Arlo yelled.

He rushed back into the room and slammed the door. Realizing he was trapped, he began thinking of how to escape. There was no way he could fight John's soldiers.

He quickly ran to the window. Just as he tried to reach out to open it, his whole body became numb. He couldn't move.

"Mom!" he screamed. "Dad!"

But no one responded.

Arlo's body started swaying. Suddenly his midsection felt like gelatin, and he couldn't hold himself upright. His knees began trembling, and his breathing became shallow.

"No! Please!"

Arlo fell backward and his head hit the edge of the bed, contorting half his body into a painful position.

"AAAAAAHHHHH!"

Suddenly the door swung open. The two boys were standing in the hallway with the same strange, grotesque smiles Arlo had seen in the museum. Their glowing emerald eyes grew bright and then dulled with each breath they took. One of the boys raised his hand in Arlo's direction, and Arlo's body rose into the air. The teenager then spread his fingers, and Arlo's legs and arms spread out as if he were on an operating table.

"Please don't do this! What do you want?" Arlo attempted to ask but his tongue failed him; a gurgling noise was all that came from his throat as he tried to speak. His two captors didn't talk. Instead, they moved closer, their neon green eyes flickering in excitement while their hideous smiles grew more swollen, oozing black fluid. Arlo tried mightily to free himself but couldn't. He began thinking of his parents, wondering if they were going through the same thing.

Suddenly the other boy opened his wooden box, revealing a stainless-steel sickle. He moved to Arlo's side and raised the blade into the air. Arlo squeezed his eyes shut and tried screaming, but nothing came out. The monster made two slicing motions, and Arlo felt a pinching, burning feeling on his hip that radiated through his stomach. He opened his eyes and looked down at his side; the skin was peeled away like an orange, dangling, dripping blood all over the floor.

Next, the other teenager opened his box, revealing long silver tongs and an oblong metal container. The boy pressed the container with his finger, and it opened. What Arlo saw next made him want to scream again; inside the box were two translucent snake-like creatures with sharp metallic teeth, snapping and biting at one another. The boy grabbed one of the monsters with the tongs and moved close to Arlo's open wound. Arlo tried with all his might to break free, but all he could do was drool. The boy inserted the creature deep inside the gash in Arlo's side and stepped back. Arlo felt the creature crawl into his belly, biting his flesh as it moved. He began coughing, and soon blood was pouring from his mouth. Arlo felt an icy sensation rush through his body and started shivering again—not from fear but from being cold. It felt like Arlo was dying, and there was nothing he could do about it. Drowsiness came next, and Arlo could barely keep his eyes open. His last vision was of the two hideous boys smiling with their ghoulish mouths, whispering to one another in celebration of their success. Arlo finally closed his eyes, and the world melted away.

21

Transitions

"Arlo! Get up!"

Jaime walked into the room and slapped his son on the head.

"What's going on? This room is a goddamned mess!"

Arlo rubbed his head and sat up to look around.

"What? Dad?"

Jaime walked over to the window and kicked the pile of blankets.

"Did you have a nightmare or something? Why are the blankets in the middle of the floor?"

Arlo remembered last night and immediately reached for his side; his waist felt normal. He looked down to inspect his side more closely; everything seemed normal, and the opening in his side was gone. Arlo looked at his dad, confused. Had he imagined it all? Was it just a bad nightmare?

"Well?" asked Jaime.

"Well, what?" asked Arlo, confused.

Jaime shook his head and walked out the door.

"Get up and clean this room before coming downstairs. If your mom sees this, she'll put you on punishment forever."

Arlo climbed out of bed and walked to the mirror on his dresser. He inspected his midsection more closely. He couldn't believe last night had been a dream.

"It seemed so real," he mumbled as he pinched his skin and saw it snap back into place. Could he have just imagined it all?

"Arlo!" his mother yelled from downstairs. "Get up!"

"I'm up!" Arlo responded.

He walked to the pile of blankets and picked them up. He was about to carry them to the bed when he paused to look at the blinds. He yanked the string on the center window and lifted the blind to inspect the glass—there was no sign of insects. Satisfied, Arlo let the blinds fall.

"I guess it was a dream," he whispered.

Arlo began making his bed when he heard a tiny knock on his bedroom door.

"I'm awake. Come in!" yelled Arlo as he walked into his bathroom.

His mother walked into the bedroom and stood at the entrance.

"Just making sure you're awake."

"Yeah, I'm about to shower."

Claire covered her nose and began backing out of the room.

"Jesus, Arlo. Close the door the next time you use the bathroom."

Arlo looked confused.

"What do you mean?"

"I know you want to take a dump with the bathroom door open, but that smell stays in your bedroom. Make sure you open all the windows before you come down."

"I didn't take a dump."

"No? Did you pass gas?"

"No."

"Really?"

"I didn't, Mom."

"Something stinks to high hell in here. Give me your linen, and I'll take it down for a wash."

"But . . ."

Arlo paused, remembering the awful smell he'd encountered last night.

"What is it?" asked Claire.

Arlo walked over to his bed and grabbed the linen. He placed the linen against his face and breathed deeply. Almost immediately, the nauseous feeling returned.

"Here, Mom. Take it," he said, pushing the pile of bed coverings into her hands.

Claire took the sheets and quickly exited the room. Arlo closed his bedroom door and flopped down on his bed as soon as she was gone. Slowly the sick feeling in his stomach went away. Arlo laid back on his sheetless bed and closed his eyes. He didn't know what to believe. As he laid there trying to make sense of what happened, he slowly drifted off to sleep for the second time.

22

Arlo's Dream

BANG. BANG. BANG. BANG.

Arlo woke to a loud pounding coming from downstairs. Someone was at the front door. He waited for one of his parents to answer the door, but the banging continued. He walked out of his bedroom and leaned over the railing.

"Mom! Dad!" Arlo yelled.

Neither of his parents answered. Arlo bounded down the stairs as the noise continued.

BANG. BANG. BANG. BANG.

"Hold your horses! I'm coming!"

Arlo opened the door and saw his father standing there.

"Dad. I'm sorry, I was about to come down to catch the bus to school. Did you forget something?"

Jaime didn't look at Arlo. Instead, he seemed to look through him with a cold, empty expression on his face.

"Dad?" asked Arlo, sensing something was wrong. "Is everything okay?"

Finally, Jaime looked into Arlo's eyes and smiled.

"I've been a good father to you, haven't I?"

"I don't get it. What do you mean?"

Jaime smiled and continued speaking.

"Do you remember when you and I made slushies for the first time? You were just a little tyke. I tried to warn you to slow down, but you couldn't because it was the first time you tasted that cherry slushie."

Arlo started feeling nervous. His father's behavior seemed like he was sleepwalking and unaware of what he was saying. His words seemed fake, like his father was reading them from a script. His mannerisms were unnatural, too; his father's head jerked when he spoke, and his movements seemed mechanical, like a robot, like someone was accessing his memory without his consent.

"I don't understand, Dad. Where is this coming from? Where's Mom?"

"You ate and ate until you began trembling uncontrollably. Do you remember that? I tried to take that icy from you, but you weren't having it. You cried until you forced me to give it back to you. And there you sat, on the porch, shivering and stuffing your mouth with ice until that stuff was gone. Do you remember that?"

Arlo responded to his father's recollection with a forced smile.

"Yeah, I remember."

"We had plenty of good times. And through it all, your mom and I did our best to love and protect you, didn't we?"

"Are you trying to tell me something? Are you and Mom getting a divorce? Where is she?"

Jaime reached out and rubbed his son's head.

"Once a man, twice a baby," he said robotically. "One day, you'll have to take care of your mother and me."

Arlo didn't understand why, but the last statement from his father comforted him. It felt like a huge weight lifted from his shoulders, and Arlo breathed a sigh of relief.

"So you're not getting a divorce? Cool. You had me worried for a minute there."

At that moment, a faint popping noise sounded, and Jaime flinched. He tried speaking again, but he started stuttering.

"Th-th-th-th-th-there is a . . ."

Jaime's stuttering startled his son, and Arlo backed away from him. Suspecting the worst, he began frantically looking around. Jaime turned away from Arlo and walked out into the yard. Smiling strangely, he looked up into the sky before turning back to Arlo.

"When he approaches you, remember what we discussed."

"I don't get it. Who are you talking about?"

Jaime laughed.

"You were never good with patience, were you, son? Don't worry. He'll be along directly."

Suddenly Arlo heard an old screen door open and slam shut. He looked past his father and saw their elderly neighbor across the street, Mrs. Gatchalian, walk out of her house carrying a lawn chair. Although the chair was small and made of aluminum, the heavyset woman struggled, breathing heavily and snorting until she dragged the chair to the center of her lawn. Satisfied with the chair's position, Mrs. Gatchalian looked up at the sun, wiped the sweat from her forehead, and began disrobing. When all her clothes were gone, Arlo gasped in surprise—just below her enormous, sagging breasts was a huge hole straight through her midsection. Flies swarmed the woman and covered her wrinkled body in seconds. But Mrs. Gatchalian remained unfazed and calmly sat down, mounds of excess skin and fat pouring over the edges of the chair. Slowly she turned her head toward Arlo and sneered, causing Arlo to jump; the old woman's facial features were different than her normal appearance; now she wore the same oversized, sponge-like, disfigured smile Arlo had seen on the two boys. Mrs. Gatchalian's eyes widened when she saw Arlo watching her, and the old woman began growling like a dog.

Suddenly the sun disappeared behind strange black clouds, and everything became as dark as night. A strong wind began blowing, but instead of the gusts pushing randomly in different directions, they seemed to pull everything toward the old woman. Arlo grabbed the railing on the porch and held himself in place. Meanwhile, the storm whipped the old woman's hair wildly, revealing large spots of missing hair on her skull. Soon thick black liquid started pouring from her mouth, and Mrs. Gatchalian began coughing uncontrollably. Finally, her eyes met Arlo's, and she let out a terrifying cackle.

"Hahahahaha!" she laughed. "Behold! I will corrupt your seed and spread dung upon your faces!" her deep, scratchy voice blared, sounding like two people speaking at once.

Arlo looked at his father standing in the center of the yard. Although the wind was strong and was pulling everything toward the old woman, Jaime stood upright, barely affected by the storm.

"Dad!" Arlo yelled. "Let's go inside!"

The woman continued yelling into the storm. Suddenly thick neon veins appeared on her face and neck, illuminating her whole body in an eerie glow that sent chills through Arlo. He covered his ears as Mrs. Gatchalian screamed louder and louder.

"AND THOU SHALT EAT THE FRUIT OF THINE OWN BODY, THE FLESH OF THY FATHERS AND MOTHERS!"

Arlo ran into the yard and grabbed his father by the arm.

"Let's get out of here, Dad!"

Jaime turned to his son and spoke calmly.

"You know I never wanted you, right?"

Arlo paused and released his father's arm.

"What?"

"That's right. Having you was your mother's idea because I didn't want you. Everything was always about what she wanted and her goddamned feelings. Forget what's best for me. I should've left the both of you years ago."

Arlo's mouth fell open, and he stared at his father in disbelief.

"Why— Why are you saying this?"

Jaime gave a chuckle that sounded robotic, and smiled.

"Oh, don't be surprised, boy. You'll know that feeling soon enough. There's nothing worse than wasting your life on a kid you never wanted and a woman that gets uglier by the day."

Arlo started sobbing. He'd never heard his father say such hurtful things.

"You son of a bitch!" he yelled.

Jaime seemed to look past his son and continued speaking.

"I never gave a shit about you or that old hag of a wife. Do you know her mom tried to pay me to go away? Do you believe that? And I, like a goddamned dummy, ignored that payday to try and do the righteous thing. I regret the day I didn't take your grandmother up on that offer. I could be with some chick in another country, sipping tequilas for years instead of wasting my life on you two."

Arlo was about to speak when something struck the top of his head. He reached up to touch his head and winced in pain—he could tell there was a deep gash in his skull. Arlo looked at his hand, expecting to see blood, and screamed again—dozens of maggots were crawling from his palm up his arm. Arlo frantically shook the creatures off his hand and looked up; instead of rain, the sky was on fire, molten stones raining down upon them, like a storm from hell.

"There's only one way to save them!" screamed Mrs. Gatchalian from her yard. Soon burning stones of fire began falling like rain, igniting the trees and causing houses to burst into flame. But Mrs. Gatchalian remained in her lawn chair, cackling and howling widely, screaming like a banshee.

"WEEEEEEE . . . You stupid son of a bitch! LET THE FIRE COME FOR THEM! I DON'T GIVE A SHIT!" she yelled. Her wild eyes locked on Arlo's, and she flashed another wicked, toothless grin at the boy.

"DO YOU HAVE THE POWER TO SAVE YOUR PARENTS?" she continued.

Arlo was terrified—the neon red veins in Mrs. Gatchalian's face radiated down her neck and throughout her large frame. Soon he could see her eyes turning green.

Sensing Arlo's fear and thoroughly enjoying it, Mrs. Gatchalian became wilder, kicking her legs and yanking at her gray hair.

"I'LL BET YOU DON'T HAVE THE BALLS TO SAVE THEM, DO YOU? THE DAY OF HELL IS COMING! WHAT ARE YOU GOING TO DO ABOUT IT? HAHAHAHA!"

Several tiny embers fell on Mrs. Gatchalian's head as she sat flailing in the chair, lighting a few strands of her gray hair. Unafraid and barely noticing the flames, she swatted at her burning hair like it was nothing more than an annoyance, and continued antagonizing Arlo.

"THEY WILL EAT THEM!" she yelled. "YOU ONLY HAVE ONE CHANCE!"

At that moment, a sizeable flaming stone shot from the sky and smashed into Mrs. Gatchalian's face, knocking her head back and partially decapitating her. Her body remained sitting in the chair while her head dangled on a thick clump of cartilage, the stone burning the center of her face.

"Dad! Mrs. Gatchalian just . . ."

Arlo was so out of breath he couldn't finish his sentence. He couldn't comprehend what was happening and began taking inventory of the things he didn't recognize; the nasty odor he'd smelled at the museum was gone, replaced by fumes so toxic, they made his eyes burn. He didn't see any of John's minions, either.

A bout of coughing struck Arlo, and he struggled to catch his breath. He now recognized the odor—sulfur fumes. He remembered what he'd learned in church, and he panicked. The world was ending, and he didn't know if he and his father would survive.

His thoughts turned to Manuel. He tried looking down the street to Manuel's house, but the smoke was too thick; everything was burning, and he was trapped.

Arlo looked to his father in desperation. He longed for his father to lead him, tell him where to hide, and how to protect himself from this hellish nightmare. But as he watched the orange embers sparkle in his father's eyes, Arlo knew his father was incapable of such actions; Jaime was but an empty shell of himself, and if Arlo wanted to survive, he had to take charge.

Suddenly a familiar muffled voice rose from the chaos—it was Mrs. Gatchalian. She'd miraculously survived and was attempting to yell out. Arlo squinted through the smoke and saw her in the same mutilated state, clinging to life.

"SSSS . . . KILL THEM. . . . IT'S TOO LATE! SHHHH . . . . ."

Finally, her body fell from the chair, and the stone in the center of her face rolled away. Arlo gasped as he saw what remained of the woman—a crushed skull with a deep indentation in her face that made her bloody eyes protrude like snail antennas, brain matter oozing from the open wounds in her head. A long purple tongue twisted in the air like a snake, gurgling and hissing, trying to formulate words formed by her damaged brain.

"SSSS . . . THE ONLY WAY . . . SHHHH . . . TO SAVE . . . KILL!"

Suddenly her head burst into flame, melting away her skin until nothing but a skull remained.

Arlo reached out and grabbed his father's arm.

"Dad! We've got to get out of here!"

Jaime remained in his robotic daze, barely acknowledging the world of fire around them. He flashed his fake smile to his son and didn't move.

"If I die, I fucking die. At least I'll be rid of you and your annoying goddamned mother," said Jaime.

Arlo ignored his father's ramblings and began pulling him across the burning yard.

"Dad! Come on!" yelled Arlo, tugging on his father's sleeve.

Several flaming stones struck Jaime's shoulders, and his shirt began burning. Arlo slapped at the garment until he extinguished the fire. He grabbed his father by his collar and pulled him through the showering fire until they reached the front of the house. Just as they were about to run onto the porch, the ground gave way, and an enormous chasm opened up beneath them. Arlo immediately reached out and grabbed a hold of the edge of the porch while his father tumbled down.

"Dad!" Arlo screamed.

Arlo looked down, and what he saw took his breath away—there was a whole world of fire beneath them: enormous burning mountains with millions of people clambering over one another to try to reach the world above them. He watched in astonishment as a huge mountain covered with thousands of people crumbled and fell into an ocean of lava. But the people that had been on the volcanic structure didn't die. Instead, they all screamed in agony as their bodies melted, regenerated, and then melted again, repeating their torture continuously as they fought to escape the ocean of pain.

"Arlo! I'm free!" screamed Jaime.

But Arlo could only watch as his father fell helplessly into the hands of a woman that was missing half her face. Jaime looked up at his son and then turned and kissed the woman romantically, her enormous tongue escaping the hole in her face and wrapping around his neck as the two kissed passionately amongst the flames. They stopped kissing, and Jaime looked up at his son and smiled again before falling into the arms of a man who bit off a piece of his forehead before pushing him aside. Jaime kept tumbling from stranger to stranger, some of them thrusting him away unharmed, while others violently protested his impeding their path to freedom.

An elderly man reached out for Jaime and wrapped his arms around his neck.

"Please! Help me!" the man screamed through tears.

Jaime pushed the man's hands away, and another group of people grabbed him.

"You son of a bitch!" yelled a teenage girl. "Let me up! You had your life!"

Another woman bit into Jaime's face, and tore away a mouthful of his cheek.

"Get out of my way!" she barked, her eyes bleeding, pink foam pouring from her mouth.

"AHHHHGGG!" screamed Jaime, his eyes locking on Arlo's.

Arlo held onto the railing, reaching out to his father, but he could do nothing.

"DADDY!" he cried. "I'M SORRY!"

At that moment, Arlo felt a hand on the collar of his shirt pull him up. It was his mother, Claire.

"Come on, Arlo. Let's go inside," said Claire.

But Arlo was beside himself.

"LET ME GO! I HAVE TO SAVE DAD!" he screamed.

Arlo watched as his father tumbled from one group to the next until he disappeared beneath a mountain of people.

"DADDY! DADDY!" he screamed.

"He's gone, baby," said Claire, pulling Arlo onto the porch.

Arlo collapsed in his mother's arms.

"I've got to save him. I can't just let him go."

Claire lifted her son and pulled him toward the door.

"You can't save him that way."

"But . . . we have to try."

"There's another way you can save him."

Arlo stopped in his tracks.

"What?"

"There's another way. John's way."

Arlo snatched his arm away from his mom.

"John? How do you know about John?"

Claire reached out for her son's arm.

"Come on, baby. Let's go in the house."

"No."

"Don't you want to save us?"

Arlo noticed his mother was starting to become nervous. Her eyes shifted back and forth from the door to him.

"Let's go inside. Come on."

Arlo took Claire's hand and moved closer to the door. As soon as she reached out, the door opened, and Arlo's mouth fell open—it was Manuel.

"What are you two doing out in this weather?" he asked.

The boy went to Arlo's mother and began caressing her hair and brushing dust from her clothing. Next, he moved to Arlo. After licking his thumb, Manuel started wiping a smudge off his friend's cheek.

Arlo could do nothing but stare. The way Manuel was moving, his words, something wasn't right. Although this person looked like his best friend, he knew this wasn't Manuel; this person seemed—old.

"Guess what? I have a nice surprise for you. I've made your favorite dessert—apple pie. If you two finish everything on your plates, I'll cut you a big slice. How does that sound?"

Claire smiled and was about to walk into the house when Arlo grabbed her arm.

"Wait," Arlo said suspiciously. "Something's not right."

"Come on in! You two will catch a cold out there."

Arlo held his mother's arm and stepped away from the door.

"We're not going inside."

Claire turned to Arlo and frowned.

"Why not? I want to go inside," she said, mimicking a child. "I want some apple pie!"

"Come on, Mom. Let's get out of here," replied Arlo.

Manuel's smile disappeared, and his body stiffened.

"Are you not coming in? Suit yourself. This old hag doesn't love you, anyway."

Manuel stepped back and lifted his arm—he was holding a gun. He pointed the weapon at the center of Claire's forehead and broke into hysterical laughter.

"You couldn't save your father, and you can't save her."

"Nooooo!" screamed Arlo.

But he was too late. Claire's head exploded, spraying blood everywhere.

23

Awakening

"No!"

Arlo sat up in bed and looked around the room.

"Manuel?" he whispered, rubbing his eyes.

He quickly looked at the alarm clock on his nightstand and saw that only five minutes had passed since he'd closed his eyes.

"But how?" he asked, confused.

At that moment, his father stuck his head in the room.

"Why aren't you dressed? I know your mother told you to get up."

Arlo didn't understand why but he suddenly felt furious at his father. The man's presence made him want to curse and scream—he longed to attack his father.

Arlo held his breath and pushed it down deep inside. Eventually, he suppressed his anger and remained silent. He rose from the bed and walked to the closet.

"I'll be ready in five minutes, Dad. I just dozed off."

"Did you stay up last night talking to that girl?"

Once again, the anger yanked at Arlo's aggression, tugging it and daring him to attack his father. Arlo remembered the cowardly image of his dream, his father falling into the abyss of the feckless horde of parents, abandoning their responsibilities in their descent to hell.

"Fucking coward," Arlo mumbled.

"What was that?" asked Jaime, watching his son closely. "What did you say?"

"I said no, Dad. I wasn't on the phone all night."

Jaime made a disgusted face and waved the air in front of his face.

"Something stinks to high hell in here. Do you have diarrhea or something? Are you sick?"

Sliding into his shirt, Arlo paused and sniffed under his arms.

"It's not me, Dad."

"When you come home today, you'll have to clean this room with soap and bleach. Do you hear me?"

"Yes, Dad."

Jaime quickly looked at his watch.

"You'll need to hurry if you want me to drop you off at school. I'll wait five minutes and not a second more."

As soon as his father was gone, a sense of dread overcame Arlo; he felt like a child too youthful and inexperienced in navigating life. The blinders were off, and he was starting to see everything clearly for the first time. The world was evil and old. Everyone around him seemed to take advantage of children in their self-serving ways. And although Arlo loved his parents, he had to admit there was a certain cynicism in their behavior toward him. Sometimes they punished him without considering the reason. Their punishments, and justifications for them, sometimes seemed excessive and heavy-handed, making Arlo feel like a young green tomato slowly roasting on hot pavement.

"Maybe they don't love me," whispered Arlo as he slid into his shoes.

The words instantly startled Arlo, and he jumped in surprise. The undercurrent of despair was unmistakable, and he knew they weren't his own. His parents had only been kind and supportive of him.

Nervously, he searched the room. Were the two boys present? Was it something else? The odor that his parents complained of was gone—Arlo couldn't smell anything.

"What's going on? It must fucking John," he mumbled, grabbing his backpack.

As he bounded down the stairs, the dreams were fresh in his head: the decapitated neighbor, his father's descent into hell, Manuel murdering his mother—it all came back. Arlo knew his world was changing. John was becoming more assertive, imposing his will on Arlo's dreams, and soon John wouldn't limit his control to the dream world. Soon he would try to take away Arlo's life and everything in it.

24

Guessing the Know

Jaime sped recklessly through traffic without speaking a word to his son. At first, Arlo thought it was because his father was late for a meeting. But when they stopped at a traffic light, and Jaime rolled down all the windows, Arlo knew the truth—his father smelled the odor from his bedroom on him.

Jaime took a sip from his coffee and looked elsewhere as if avoiding the odor. Meanwhile, Arlo stared at his father in utter contempt, a thunderous rage building inside. The visions of the hellish nightmare came rushing back—that pathetic, emasculated expression painted on his father's face as he fell to the burning earth.

Arlo audibly sucked his teeth and shook his head in disgust. He didn't realize it before, but his father was an arrogant asshole who thought he was better than everything and everyone, from how he made Arlo's mother iron his dress socks to how he made her verbally confirm his lame breakfast menu each night. Arlo rolled his eyes at his father while chewing over his father's annoying habits.

Damn, this guy is lame. He's been eating the same boring-ass breakfast for as long as I can remember. But he's making her call out the menu like he's a drill sergeant? Like we're having people over for breakfast? What a goddamned pile of shit.

Arlo detested how his father behaved like the world was only for him, and everyone had to do his bidding. The dream was fresh in Arlo's mind, like an itchy mosquito bite he couldn't scratch. He felt the hatred toward his father growing with every breath.

As Jaime turned the corner on the road to the school, he looked over at his son and caught his derision, yet remained silent. The boy didn't care because his thoughts of his father were brimming with hostility.

So what if he says something? I don't give a fuck. He's lucky I don't grab the wheel and run this car into the nearest two-ton truck.

A fucking loser. What kind of man couldn't protect his wife and son? That son of a bitch would leave us dead at the first opportunity. Go ahead and kill yourself, you scumbag.

When Jaime pulled up in front of the school to drop off his son, Arlo found himself struggling to breathe. Hatred was smothering him inside the car, and he wanted out.

Jaime didn't speak to his son. Instead, he revved the engine and sped off, barely allowing Arlo to shut the car door.

"Fucking prick," Arlo muttered as he turned away from the curb.

Arlo was at the end of the sidewalk when his father's car disappeared in traffic. His anger seemed to melt away as soon as his dad was gone, and he could breathe again.

Feeling better, Arlo began searching for Manuel. Frantically he searched the crowd of students lingering by the curb, but Manuel wasn't there. Arlo's eyes darted face to face, hoping to see Manuel running his mouth to one of the other boys about sports—still, he wasn't there. Arlo sighed in frustration.

"Where are you, Mani?" he asked as he looked at his wristwatch. Could the ghostly twins have gotten him? Did John kill him in his dream?

Suddenly Arlo's stomach growled loudly, and he lurched forward in pain.

"I can't take this shit," he complained as he rubbed his belly. "Where are you, Manuel?"

His mind began speeding through potential reasons for his friend's absence: Maybe the ghostly twins had visited him, or perhaps John had come to his house and taken him away.

Before Arlo could think of any other reason for Manuel's absence, the school bell rang, and the children began filing into the building. As each student passed, Arlo scanned their faces again in search of the boy. But after a few minutes, he shrugged, threw his backpack over his shoulder, and went into the building.

25

And You, Too

Arlo didn't see Manuel until the bell rang for the second period. When he came out of class, Arlo spotted him exiting his classroom.

"Manuel!" yelled Arlo.

But the boy didn't hear him. Instead, Manuel walked through the hall like a stiff piece of wood caught in the current of a stream, banging into students without acknowledging them. Arlo didn't yell again, instead preferring to speak directly with Manuel.

As the two boys drew closer, Arlo noticed that Manuel wasn't himself; enormous bags were under his bloodshot eyes, and dried saliva was in the corners of his mouth. His clothing was wrinkled, and the laces of his shoes dangled on the floor.

"Shit," said Arlo as he approached him. As soon as he was close enough, Arlo reached out and grabbed Manuel's arm.

"Hey," said Arlo, pulling Manuel close. "We need to talk."

Manuel stopped and turned his head. As soon as he saw Arlo's face, his eyes widened.

"Yeah. We have to talk. Meet me on the bleachers at lunchtime."

Manuel continued to his class while Arlo stood watching his friend as he walked away. He'd never seen him behave in such a way. Manuel looked almost like a walking zombie with his unkempt appearance, pale skin, and bloodshot eyes. As Manuel stumbled down the hall and disappeared, Arlo walked down the hallway and entered his next class.

Sitting close to the window, Arlo watched as the other students began stumbling into the room. He didn't know how he would make it through the class. Arlo was exhausted—more than just tired, he was genuinely spent; his eyelids felt as heavy as stones while his muscles ached, like Arlo had been playing football all day. And on top of those issues, he was starving, as though he hadn't eaten anything for two days.

Suddenly a loud, long growl sounded from Arlo's belly, and he jumped, hoping no one heard the noise. Other than one boy who cast a curious glance in his direction, the chattering of the incoming students drowned out the hunger noise.

Arlo cupped his chin in his palm and stared out the window. The light was shining, but the world seemed darker, like someone unscrewed the sun bulb and replaced it with a dim, low-wattage bulb. Arlo could see a few birds flying outside, but they all seemed to be moving slower, almost off rhythm with normality. Everything was a step behind what he usually saw, existing in his delayed world, trapped by the logic of the life he'd lived before and this new world, now that he was aware of something more sinister.

A few girls entered the classroom and sat down at the desks closest to Arlo.He paid attention briefly, stirred by their conversation. They were gossiping about Nathan Cooper's accident, giggling and jumbling the story as they retold what a friend of a cousin's friend heard. When the teacher came into the classroom, the girls' story about Nathan Cooper was drastically different: A gang member from out of town had shot the boy.

Arlo chuckled and listened to the teacher perform her roll call. After he responded to his name, the lull of the teacher's voice added to the heaviness on his eyelids, and Arlo dozed off.

26

Dreaming of John

It wasn't raining, but the forest was wet, like a fresh storm had passed. Arlo could hear the gentle dripping of water as he walked, and the sound was soothing. He walked past an enormous, leafy plant, swiped at it, and wiped the water on his face.

"Life should always be like this," he said with a smile. He began searching his memory for other moments that made him feel at peace. Suddenly Arlo flashed a wide grin. He didn't understand how he remembered, but the wet forest reminded him of when he was a baby—when his mother used to tap his cheek with her soft fingertips, humming gently in his ear to coax him to sleep. Arlo imagined his mother's voice as he walked through the forest. He longed to have her close, to share nature's beauty with her. She was the only person with whom he felt a genuine connection. His imagination took over, and it wasn't long before Arlo began hearing her soft voice singing.

"Arleeee . . . Arleeee. God's kiss to meeee."

Arlo smiled. His mother's soft voice tickled the leaves above him, and he knew she was there. A sense of peace moved through him, warming him with memories of his mother's warm smile as she looked down at him while she breastfed. Occasionally a drop of water would land on Arlo's head and trickle down his back. He fancied the rain a kiss from his mother, the cool liquid caressing his skin, washing away the world's stresses.

"I know you're here, Mom," said Arlo as he wiped the water from his neck. Arlo breathed deeply. The whole forest held her scent—that sweaty, baby-oiled smell after she'd worked cleaning the homes of wealthy people all day. Missing his mother and feeling her presence everywhere, Arlo spoke aloud.

"I miss you, too, Mom. Are you here? I can smell you."

But Arlo was alone in the forest, and the only response he received was the light trickle of water falling from the trees. He looked up and was mesmerized by the rays of sunshine coming through the trees; the brightness of the light and the rising fog gave the forest a mystical glow. The scent of exotic shrubbery tickled Arlo's nose, but he breathed deeply and smiled, continuing his trek into the woods.

Arlo was enjoying the solitude of his journey. There were no annoying sounds from the city, nor did he need to fear wildlife. It wasn't that the rain chased all wildlife away. Arlo felt in his element because the forest felt like a place where no problem could touch him—only beauty.

But . . .

Suddenly Arlo began hearing something in the forest—the sound of a large group of people chanting. The noise startled him, and he began looking around.

"What's going on? What is that?" he asked.

As Arlo moved through the forest, the chanting grew louder, angering Arlo and making his eye spasm. Annoyed, he rubbed his eyes and searched the woods.

"Where are they?" he asked.

Arlo tried escaping the noise by walking in different directions, but the noise grew louder, no matter where he turned. Arlo grew angrier, and his frustration made him sweat. He wiped at his forehead but continued perspiring uncontrollably. Soon his whole body was wet, and Arlo had to remove his shirt. He tossed it aside and fanned his arms, hoping to catch a nice breeze. But nothing could stop the unrelenting heat from bearing down on him. With each step, the forest grew more humid, becoming hotter as the chants became louder. The sound was pollution to Arlo's ears, and he detested it.

"Like fucking flies at a picnic," he mumbled. "Where is that shit coming from?" he asked, pushing through the forest.

But now the forest was more treacherous, and Arlo could barely see where he was walking. He stumbled over stones, and thick briars scratched his legs. The mystical beauty of the forest was gone, replaced by foreboding darkness that cast a shadow over Arlo's soul. The atmospheric change seemed to awaken all the forest at once; crickets began singing loudly, and gnats attacked Arlo from all around. Still, Arlo continued toward the source of the chants.

Soon Arlo arrived at an enormous bush and stopped. It was a peculiar shrub; its leaves were orange, casting a scent in the air that smelled like black licorice.

"I always hated that stuff," mumbled Arlo as he reached out to one of the leaves. His fingertips began burning as soon as he touched it, and Arlo quickly wiped his hand on his pants. When he lifted his hand to inspect his fingertips, he was surprised to see that his thumb and pinky were missing; the only thing remaining in their places were stumps of bloody meat. The gruesome sight didn't surprise Arlo because there was no pain. Calmly, he held his hand up and looked at the dangling pieces of meat with derision, chucking as he thought his fingerless hand resembled raw, mangled chicken fingers from his favorite restaurant. Slowly, he backed away from the strange plant and began looking on the ground for his missing appendages.

Suddenly the bush started moving, shaking slightly at first and then thrashing violently back and forth. Terrified, he waited for whatever was there to reveal itself.

It must be a raccoon or a boar.

That is what Arlo told himself, but the truth was that he knew something was hunting him, watching, waiting for the right moment to attack. The fear of not knowing what was watching him shook Arlo more than anything. At that moment, he became astutely aware of his vulnerability; he was a young boy alone in the forest, a place with menacing, hungry creatures capable of extinguishing his life. There was no light, only the certainty of peril hiding within the shadows of darkness. The joyous feeling Arlo enjoyed was gone. There were no rays of sunshine to light his path—only the night. And that darkness signaled the arrival of something terrible—something evil.

Arlo's stomach began hurting, and he rubbed it as he watched the bush, hoping whatever was in it would leave. But then . . . something in the bush started growling. Fearing for his safety, Arlo knelt and picked up a stone. He wanted to believe that the sounds belonged to a pig or a wolf. But the deep, throaty, aggressive growls told him something much more powerful was there, gnashing its teeth as it hungrily watched Arlo from behind the bush.

"Hey!" he yelled nervously. "Get back!"

Without thinking, Arlo hurled the stone into the bush. The growling stopped, and he felt relieved. Arlo was about to continue his pursuit of the chanting voices when suddenly a thunderous growling came from everywhere, encircling him, protesting his unprovoked aggression. The sounds seemed to intensify Arlo's stomach pain, and he doubled over in agony.

After listening for a few moments more, Arlo found an opening—there was no growling from the bushes closest to him. Arlo took off running. He could hear the creatures pursuing him, ripping apart trees as they gave chase. Arlo's stomach was killing him; the pain radiated through his side and up his spine, but he ignored it and continued his reckless run through the darkness.

Realizing he should try to throw the animals off his trail, Arlo ran through several large bushes, ducked behind large trees, and dove head-first into a giant briar patch. As the needles stripped away the skin from his back, Arlo almost screamed.

And all the while, the chanting grew louder.

Finally, Arlo arrived on the edge of a field of tall grass. He was about to enter when he noticed a clear sticky substance on the plants.

"Shit. Spider webs," Arlo whispered as he shuddered. He hated spiders more than anything; he'd always had nightmares of the bugs crawling into his mouth and ears as he slept. Now he was face-to-face with hundreds of them.

Suddenly the trees behind him shook, sending a group of sleeping crows scattering into the night sky. Arlo's heart pounded, and he shrunk closer to the ground, trying to evade what was approaching. Suddenly a ferocious growl rose from the darkness, and several trees near him fell to the ground. Arlo decided he could wait no longer and swiped at the spiderweb in front of him, and ran through the bushes. His eyes filled with tears as he moved through the weeds; spiders were crawling all over his sweaty skin, clinging to his neck and back, searching for a place to dig their sharp fangs into his skin. But Arlo didn't have time to stop and wipe the bugs away. Something much worse was coming.

The chants were getting louder, and Arlo ran toward the voices. Maybe someone in the group would help him evade what was hunting him. Arlo turned left and sprinted, weeds smacking his face; he stopped for a moment and listened.

"They're near," he whispered, then sprinted again.

Suddenly Arlo burst from the tall grass and looked around. There was a clearing up ahead with a strange purple light shining. Arlo looked behind him, trying to locate his pursuer, but no one was there. Satisfied that he'd gotten away, he inched closer to the clearing while maintaining his cover behind trees. He could feel the chants vibrating the ground now—a strange language he'd never heard before.

"Talom kandura madrinko. Talom kandura madrinko. We are here to serve you, Balam."

Arlo tiptoed to a large tree and slowly peeked out from behind. Standing on the other side was a circle of people naked and covered in mud. The purple light lit up their eyes like fire, each lost in a deep trance, speaking the strange words repeatedly.

"Talom kandura madrinko. Talom kandura madrinko. We are here to serve you, Balam."

In the center of the crowd was a pit filled with what appeared to be mud but smelled much worse. Suddenly a naked man walked to the hole, grabbed two handfuls of the waste, and rubbed it on his face.

"Talom kandura madrinko," he said, opening his mouth and pushing the mud inside. He gagged a bit and then swallowed, his eyes opening wide afterward. The sound of a squealing pig came from the crowd, and soon, the animal was in the strange man's hands. Someone gave the man a knife, and he cut the pig's throat, smiling as the animal thrashed about in his arms until it bled to death. After the animal stopped moving, the man decapitated the pig and disemboweled it. He passed the entrails to the nearest old woman, and she took a bite before passing the guts on to the next person.

Arlo watched the scene in disgust. His stomach was churning, moving beneath his palm as he rubbed it, trying to calm himself.

There was a slight commotion, and soon two men led a man wearing a suit and a woman wearing a tattered dress to the front. Arlo looked at the woman and could see that she was scared out of her mind. She looked like she'd been in a battle; her dress was torn and splattered with mud, and her hair was filthy. The woman was sobbing while holding what looked like a small bundle of clothing in her arms.

"You can't do this!" she yelled.

A thought shot through Arlo's mind as quickly as lightning when the baby's cries rang out. He was watching a sacrifice.

"Michael, please!" the woman screamed. "You've got to do something!"

"There, there. Everything's going to be okay, Lydia. There's nothing to worry about."

Michael was unfazed by his wife's behavior and moved closer. He gently kissed his wife's forehead and caressed the infant's cheek. When the baby stopped crying, Michael nodded to an elderly naked old woman, and stepped aside.

"You don't need to be afraid, miss. You'll see," she said, reaching out for the child. "You're the mother of a king that has come to lead us all to the glory of Talom."

Lydia snatched the child away and spat in the woman's face.

"Get away from my son, you twisted old bitch!"

The old woman smiled at Lydia and wiped the spit from her face. She paused a moment and held her fingers up for inspection. After smiling hungrily at the thick, slimy saliva hanging from her fingers, she shoved her hands into her mouth, sucking until the mucus was gone.

"You're sick!" yelled Lydia. "You're all fucking sick!"

Suddenly Lydia turned and tried to run away, but two men caught her and brought her back to the pit.

"Let go of me!" she cried.

Michael walked over to his wife and held out his hands.

"Lydia, give me our son."

"What? Never!"

"Don't you see? It's the only way."

"How could you do this, Michael? I loved you."

The two men grabbed Lydia's arms while Michael took the baby away from her and passed it to the elderly woman.

"My king," the old woman whispered, her eyes wild with anticipation. Suddenly she snatched the blanket off, grabbed the baby by his ankle, and dangled him over the pit.

"No! Please!" screamed Lydia, flailing about, trying to break free.

None of the other people said a word as the woman let go of the baby. Arlo gasped and looked away, trying to comprehend what he'd just witnessed.

Maybe he's okay. Yeah, they were joking. There's no way they could kill that child.

But when Arlo replayed the images in his mind, he knew that the child was gone. He couldn't get the dreadful event out of his mind; the innocent look on the child's face when he plunged into the filth; the excited looks on the faces of the mud people as they welcomed the baby's demise. Arlo could hear the mother of the child sobbing uncontrollably. Finally, he gathered enough strength to open his eyes again.

"Get him out!" yelled Lydia.

But her husband ignored her, looking at the pit coldly, emotionless.

Finally, one of the people passed a stone container to the elderly woman.

"It is time to bring forth the power of Talom, our savior."

The woman drank from the container until her mouth was full. Suddenly she sprayed the liquid from her mouth into the pit. She grabbed the torch from the side of the hole and tossed it in, and the whole pit burst into flame.

"Talom is here!"

With this statement, the group erupted in celebration. They danced and hugged one another as they screamed strange words into the sky. Meanwhile, Lydia sat on the ground staring into the burning pit, mourning her child, while her husband watched with his hands shoved in his pockets.

And then Arlo saw it—movement from the center of the mud. First a bubbling, and then a tiny hand breaking the surface.

"Shhhhh," the elderly woman said. "He approaches."

As everyone stood transfixed, the flames in the pit suddenly went out. A few men became terrified and took off running into the night. The others continued staring, unable to move. The baby's head inched out of the muck until its eyes, glowing red, were visible. Soon its entire head rose from the muddy waste and released a terrifying cry. The baby was hell come to life, burning inside with the fires of Hades.

Arlo's heart was racing, and he wanted to get out of there. He could see the fires of hell burning inside the baby and knew something terrible would happen, but he couldn't move; his curiosity and fear trapped him, unable to escape.

The infant's eyes fell on Lydia, and she cried out. She had been watching her baby, partly confused but mostly sad.

"John? Is that you?" she asked, reaching out to him. The baby's father took a step away from the hole with a noticeable look of fear. The baby glanced at the man before turning its attention back to Lydia.

"M-m-mommy?"

Tears poured from Lydia's face, and she turned to her husband.

"Oh, Michael. John said 'Mommy' to me for the first time."

Lydia rose to her feet and stumbled to the edge of the opening. One of her captors grabbed her arm.

"No!" he yelled, pulling her back. "The transformation is not complete!"

Both men grabbed Lydia and pulled her from the edge.

"Mommy. Mommy," the child cried as it struggled to free itself from the mud.

Suddenly, the child's hand rose from the mud and made a fist. The two men holding Lydia screamed and started trembling uncontrollably. Soon they were high in the air, struggling to free themselves from an invisible force. The baby extended its fingers, and the skin of both men ripped off their bodies like sheets on a bed, spraying everyone with their blood. The men screamed in agony, alive and pleading for help.

Meanwhile, Lydia sank to her knees, crying and laughing as she watched the gruesome bodies floating above her. She looked to her husband for help, but he ignored her and wiped the blood from his suit. Finally, she turned to the baby in the sewage.

"John!" yelled Lydia. "John! Stop it!"

Suddenly both bodies fell to the ground.

The baby struggled for a few more seconds and then sank into the filth until all signs of movement were gone.

Everyone stood breathless, watching and waiting for a sign of life. A few seconds passed, then a minute, and then five minutes—still, nothing. Eventually, chatter rose from the mud-covered spectators. They all looked at one another, trying to discern if the baby was dead. Finally, curiosity turned to anger. Several people confronted the old woman, yelling at her in their strange language. Others shook their heads in disappointment and began retreating into the dark forest while everyone ignored the two skinless men on the ground, moaning in pain.

Meanwhile, Lydia could do nothing but sit on the ground, crying. Her child was gone, and she stared into the pit, sobbing, rocking back and forth.

"Murderers . . . murderers," she repeated over and over.

Her husband stood a few steps away, staring into the pit, looking dejected, seemingly annoyed by his wife's crying. Periodically, he'd glance at the old woman and then shake his head before wiping a few drops of blood from his jacket.

Suddenly the injured men began screaming, and everyone looked at the mud. Arlo watched as the bodies of the bloody men started sliding along the ground toward the pit.

Lydia jumped to her feet.

"John! He's alive!"

The bodies of the men slid along the ground until they splashed into the sludge. Neither of them sank; instead, they floated atop the muck with their faces buried in the liquid. Eventually, the men drowned, and their bodies lay splayed out, one in front of the other, forming a bridge from the grass into the center of the pit. Soon a tiny hand appeared on the arm of one of the men and then another.

"The king arrives!" yelled the old woman with an evil, toothless smile.

The child climbed upon the corpses, thick mud dripping from its tiny body and red glowing eyes that looked like burning coals. It crawled along the bodies of the men until it reached the grass where Lydia sat.

"John! Come to Mommy," Lydia said, holding out her arms.

The demon baby flashed a sinister smile at its mother and looked at its father. The man seemed nervous and moved away from the child.

"Hey!" Michael yelled to the group of mud people. "Aren't you guys supposed to do something?"

None of them moved.

Michael looked at his son sitting in front of him and became more nervous—the boy's bloody gaze watched him closely.

"H-hey. John? Remember me? Daddy?"

The baby smiled, and a cute giggle escaped its drooling mouth. Michael felt relaxed and continued talking to the child.

"That's a good boy. Remember me?"

Suddenly the child released a terrifying demonic scream and sailed through the air, landing on Michael's chest. Michael fell backward, trying to push the child away, but the monster held on.

"HELP! SOMEONE GET THIS THING OFF ME!" Michael screamed.

But the baby wouldn't let go. It opened its mouth, revealing long, razor-sharp teeth, and bit into Michael's neck, ripping out a chunk of flesh before tumbling off the man. The demonic baby threw back its head and swallowed the meat whole. As blood sprayed from the wound in his neck, Michael tried pressing his hand against the hole to stop the bleeding. He stumbled around, trying to climb to his feet, but the child jumped on him again. This time the monster bit into the other side of Michael's neck. Michael's eyes rolled back in his head, and he fell to the ground, motionless. The baby straddled the man again and began eating him.

Arlo watched in horror as the baby ate continuously, chewing through Michael's clothes to reach the meat underneath.

"Holy shit!" Arlo exclaimed as he watched from the shadows. He didn't realize he'd said the words out loud until the baby suddenly stopped devouring the carcass. The creature slowly sat up and turned in Arlo's direction.

"Yoooooooouuuuu!" the creature screamed.

Arlo stumbled backward, falling over a tree stump as he focused on the demonic child, growling and moving toward him with hungry red eyes. When it jumped across the pit and landed a few feet beyond Arlo's hiding place, Arlo turned to sprint. As soon as he did, he froze— the baby and all the mud people stood before him, blocking his escape. Before Arlo could run in another direction, the demon baby jumped on him, lifted its head, and bit into his neck.

27

Waking in Class

"AAAAAHHHHHHHHH! Get the fuck off me!"

Arlo fell from his desk onto the floor. His eyes were closed, and he swung wildly, hoping a lucky punch would hit a few of his attackers. After a few seconds, Arlo heard giggles and whispering. But then familiar faces came into focus, all surrounding him, looking down and laughing at him as he laid on the floor.

"Is there a problem, Mr. Ortega?" a voice asked from above the fray.

Arlo was still confused, and he wasn't sure of all the faces surrounding him. Was he still in the forest? Was this an attack?

"Huh?" he asked, rubbing his eyes.

Suddenly the faces parted, and his teacher looked down at him.

"Are you comfortable, Mr. Ortega, or should I get you a pillow and blanket?"

Arlo climbed to his feet and sat at his desk.

"Good. Now, everyone, back to your seats."

Just as the other students sat down at their desks, the bell rang, and they all sprinted for the door. Feeling dizzy and confused, Arlo, too, stumbled to the door. Just as he was about to exit, the teacher spoke.

"Try to get a good night's sleep, Mr. Ortega. A few hours of sleep will prevent future nap-induced, profanity-laced classroom outbursts."

"Yes, sir."

Arlo walked out of the classroom and sprinted down the hall. He had to meet Manuel for lunch.

28

What Evil Does to Friends

When Arlo arrived at the bleachers, Manuel was already sitting there, waiting for him.

"Dude, what took you so long?"

"What do you mean? Class just let out."

"Sorry, I didn't even hear the bell. My mind is fucking tripping. I'm seeing shit that's not there, scared to go to sleep—I don't know how much longer I can keep this up."

Arlo looked at Manuel, and sat down on the bleachers beside him. Manuel's appearance was worse than when he'd passed him in the hallway. There were circular dark bruises on his face, and patches of his hair were missing. A noticeable wheeze escaped his mouth when he breathed, like someone had punched him in the stomach, and he struggled to catch his breath.

Arlo began feeling guilty. If he'd never met Isadora, none of this would be happening to Manuel. He wanted to ask Manuel about his dreams but became afraid. Who knows what kind of sick, twisted evil John used to torture Manuel?

"I know what you're thinking," said Manuel.

"What?" asked Arlo.

"You've been asking yourself the same question I have. We're going to die, aren't we?"

The question surprised Arlo, but what was more surprising was his response.

"Yeah, I think so."

Manuel sucked in the air once more and pulled out a notebook.

"Well, if I die, I'm not going without a fight."

Arlo sat up.

"What do you have?"

"Well, you know I haven't been sleeping much. I stayed awake trying to research this John dude."

"Yeah? And?"

"The closest thing I found is this guy the police nicknamed John Mudd. The police caught him a few years ago when he tried to kidnap this little girl. They had him in custody, but he broke out. To this day, they haven't caught him. And all the while, kids keep disappearing."

Arlo shook his head in disbelief.

"I don't know. That seems sketchy."

"A few kids escaped and told of their capture. The things he did to those kids is some sick shit—he does the same things to me in my dreams."

Manuel began scratching himself all over.

"Jesus! The bugs. The worms. That son of a bitch made me chop up my dad with a machete and eat his intestines in a bowl of spaghetti. Can you believe that? I swear I'll never eat spaghetti again."

Arlo shook his head in disgust. He knew how much Manuel loved spaghetti—it was his favorite meal, and John had taken what he enjoyed most and used it against him.

Manuel was shaking uncontrollably, and Arlo had to wrap his arms around the boy.

"Take it easy, Mani. Easy, bro."

Attempting to get hold of himself, Manuel shook his head and rubbed his eyes.

"I'm not cool, bro. This shit is changing me. Anyway, I came across another story that happened around the same time. This group of bank robbers escaped into the Black Hills Forest, and they all died except for one. When the police pulled him out of the woods, he told them of a family of witches that killed people. The police killed the whole family, except the son—a kid they called *John*."

"So you think the two stories are connected?"

"Yeah. The John that kidnaps children is the same John who escaped that house in the forest."

Arlo remained silent as he thought about the story.

"Well?" asked Manuel, rubbing his eyes. "What do you think?"

"There's something else."

"What?"

"I've had dreams, too."

"What does that son of a bitch make you do in your dreams? Did he make you kill your dad? Eat his guts?"

"He does horrible things to me in my dreams, but that's not the point. The nightmares seem to have one goal—to make me hate my parents. It's like he's trying to send us a message."

"Yeah—he wants to make our lives hell."

"It might go deeper than that."

"I think it does. This morning, I dreamed of my dad beating up my mom."

"Is it true?"

Feeling embarrassed, Manuel looked away before speaking.

"I've never talked about this, but more than a few times, I heard my dad beating my mom when he was drunk. Now, whenever he's been drinking, my mom takes my sister and me to my aunt's house until he passes out."

"Holy shit."

"Yep. True."

"In my dream, my father told me he didn't want me and wanted to abandon us. It was all twisted into a nightmare, but it was my father's true thoughts. I heard him and Mom fighting once when she accused him of sleeping with his secretary, and he admitted he never wanted me."

"Jesus! Are you serious?"

Tears filled Arlo's eyes, and he wiped them away.

"Yeah. That fucker, John, dug into my memories and used that pain in a nightmare."

Manuel put his arm around Arlo.

"I'd almost prefer to be dead than to live through his bullshit."

"The dream itself isn't relevant, but the overall theme is what's most important. John wants us to hate our parents."

"But why?"

"Because I think John wants us to kill them. John hates his parents. And I think it's all tied to why he takes the kids."

Manuel sighed.

"All this is good to know, but how can we use it?"

Arlo rubbed his face in frustration.

"I'm not sure. But if we hope to save ourselves from this crap, we have to find a weakness in John."

"But there's only one way for us to do that."

"I know. We're going to have to let John into our lives."

"Through sleep?"

"Yeah."

Manuel stood and rubbed his eyes.

"I don't know about that, Arlo. The things that happen in my sleep are pretty fucking scary. Sometimes I think I'm going to die. Last night those two boys showed up at my house, and I don't know if they really came or if I was dreaming."

Arlo sat up.

"The boys? What happened?"

"They put something in my stomach."

"Worms?"

"Yeah."

"Me, too."

"Then they *did* come. What are we going to do, Arlo?"

"I don't know. But tonight, you need to search the internet to see if you can find the location of John's house."

"Why? I'm not going anywhere near the place."

"We might not have a choice. Remember when you met me at the museum? John's spirit was there, but he wasn't. He's never in the dreams in physical form. I think John gives the kids his powers through witchcraft and uses them to do his bidding. But I don't think he has ever left that house in the forest. If we fight back, the house is the key."

Manuel grabbed his book bag.

"Look, I've got to get to class before one of these teachers calls my parents. About John, I guess we don't have a choice at this point. I'll try to find the house's location online, but we don't know if it's still there. The cops probably knocked it down or something. I'll search, though. But you should probably look for a weakness. None of my dreams tell me that this dude would die the traditional holy-water or fire-and-brimstone way. You've got to find his weak spot so we don't go to his house empty-handed."

As soon as Manuel turned to walk away, Arlo called out to him.

"Hey! Mani!"

"Yeah?"

"If you need help, call me."

"You, too, Arlo."

"Love you, bro."

"Ditto."

Arlo sat down on the bleachers and watched until Manuel crossed the field and disappeared. He began thinking about his friendship with Manuel. It was amazing the two had been friends for so long but had hidden their most painful secrets from one another.

Arlo stood and threw his backpack over his shoulder. Just as he was about to return to class, he paused—a sound came from the bushes behind the bleachers. Someone was crying. After his conversation with Manuel, Arlo became suspicious and wanted to run away. Was it another one of John's tricks? He tried ignoring the cries and turned to walk away.

The emotional whimpers began tugging at Arlo's curiosity. Arlo could tell it was a girl; her cries sounded like those of a small child, so frail and helpless. What if she needed his help? How could he leave without knowing if she was okay?

As Arlo walked behind the metal benches and into the dense brush, the crying grew louder, more desperate. There was a large bush in his path, and Arlo pushed past it into a clearing. He immediately covered his nose; there was a stench unlike what he'd smelled at the museum. The odor was the stench of death, and Arlo knew it. At the far end of the clearing, Arlo saw it—the carcasses of several dead cats covered in ants; a rotting boar that was missing its head, flies swarming all around it; and various textbooks and paper scattered on the ground.

In the center of the area was a sizeable leaf-covered branch, moving up and down with the sobs Arlo heard. Whoever was crying was hiding underneath. Arlo tiptoed to the leaves, grabbed the wood, and suddenly yanked it back.

It was Isadora. She growled at Arlo, her eyes colorless and devoid of life, her wrinkled, pale skin drooping on one side of her face while the other was skinless, exposing her skull.

"OH MY GOD! ISADORA!" yelled Arlo.

He fell onto his back and tried crawling away from the girl, but Isadora jumped on top of him, snapping her mouth like a wild animal as thick saliva dripped from her mouth onto Arlo's face.

"STOP! G-GET OFF ME!" screamed Arlo, the stench of rotting flesh burning his nose. He tried pushing Isadora's face away, but his thumb got stuck in her eyeball. Isadora continued snapping at his face, trying to bite him as Arlo struggled to free his thumb. Finally, Arlo pulled it out of Isadora's eye socket with her eyeball attached, causing black fluid to shoot from her eye socket into his mouth. He gagged, the liquid tasting like a rotten egg, and then vomited on himself before finally thrusting the girl aside. Arlo climbed to his feet, grabbed the nearest rock, and smashed it into the side of Isadora's head, causing the zombie's other eye to fall out. Isadora stumbled around blindly, growling and spitting putrid saliva, a strange green glow burning inside her skull. Finally, the monster sniffed the air, growled at Arlo, and took off running in the opposite direction, crashing through the trees and disappearing into the forest.

Arlo stood staring into the forest, confused by what he'd just experienced. Although their relationship was fake, he felt sorrow for Isadora. No one deserved this. He could still hear her cries in his mind, the cry of a tortured child lost in a word of death and evil. Maybe a part of her was still alive, trying to find a way out of the rotting corpse she'd become. Maybe there was something in Arlo that brought out the worst, reminding her of the broken promise from John. He knew what that felt like—to believe and then have it stripped away, leaving nothing but that feeling of betrayal.

Wiping the slime and vomit from his clothing, Arlo decided it was time for him to go home. He grabbed his bag and took off running. He had some work to do if he and Manual were to devise a way to stop John. Isadora was just a wild zombie running around mindlessly. But Arlo was sure when the time came for John to try to take his life, it wouldn't be with something so out of control.

29

Getting the Stains Out

When Arlo arrived home, he was surprised to see all his bedroom furnishings on the front lawn. His mother, a handkerchief covering her face and yellow rubber gloves on her hands, was scrubbing Arlo's dresser with a brush. Arlo walked up to his mother as she turned on the hose and sprayed the soap off the furniture.

"What are you doing?" Arlo asked.

"Oh!" exclaimed Claire. "You scared me. Why are you home so early?"

"I wasn't feeling well. My stomach's been hurting a lot lately. What are you doing?"

Arlo tried to kiss his mother, and she recoiled.

"Gosh! You smell horrible! Did you vomit on yourself?"

"Yeah. That's why I decided to come home."

"Well, hurry up and go take a shower. You reek."

"Yep."

"It's probably that smell in your room making you sick. I went in there to put your clean clothes away, and that odor was so strong I couldn't take it anymore. I decided to take everything out of your room and bleach it."

"You could've waited until I got home. I could've helped you."

"It wasn't too difficult. I just dragged everything down the stairs and out the door."

"Where's Dad?"

"He'll be home at his usual time. Are you hungry? Did you eat lunch? After you finish showering, some leftover empanadas are on the counter if your stomach can handle it."

"Nah, I'm okay. I think I'll watch some TV."

"Everything should be clean and back in your room in a few hours."

"Okay. Thanks, Mom."

Arlo walked into the house and ran upstairs to his bedroom. When he walked into his room, bleach was the first thing he smelled. But still, underneath the cleaning chemicals and the fresh air blowing into the room, Arlo could smell the stench of the museum and John's filth, hanging in the room like death in a morgue.

Arlo showered, got dressed, and went to the TV room. Watching a game show, he began thinking of Manuel and Isadora. All their lives were intertwined, each taking drastically different paths, but all would surely die. The whole thing felt strange to Arlo, like he was sitting in a car about to crash, knowing what he needed to do to avoid certain death but not being able to move quickly enough to stop it.

Arlo never heard his mother struggling to bring his furniture back into the house. His eyelids were too heavy, and he was too tired to pay attention to anything. Soon he was fast asleep.

30

The Dreams Keep Coming

Arlo burst from the bushes, sweating and out of breath. He had to cross a stream to avoid being caught. Suddenly a roar sounded from the trees, scaring Arlo so much that he fell into the water. Arlo quickly picked himself up and jumped from stone to stone, trying to reach the other side. He was almost on the other side of the stream when he fell and twisted his ankle.

"Ow! Fuck!" he yelled.

He immediately rose to his feet and climbed out of the water onto the other side. He looked back and heard the snapping of trees moving closer to his position. Arlo took off running again, breathing heavily and continuously looking back. Finally, he pushed past a large bush and stumbled onto a trail. Arlo took a moment to catch his breath and gather his bearings. He had no idea where he was or how to escape the forest.

Suddenly a great roar sounded only a few feet from his position, shaking the leaves of the trees. Arlo took off running once more. He ran through the forest, stumbling out of control while the monster's steps grew closer.

Finally, Arlo pushed through a set of small trees and stumbled onto a trail. He didn't know where the path led, but he was grateful he didn't have to battle through the clutter of the forest for a while.

"I've got to keep moving," he whispered, breathing heavily. His lungs were on fire, and he didn't know how he would continue sprinting. Arlo bent over to catch his breath. As soon as he did, a tiny whisper came from one of the bushes.

"Psst! Hey!" whispered a voice.

Arlo saw a small, frail hand motioning to him from the shadows. Cautiously, he looked behind to see if the monster trailing him was in sight before moving closer. Hidden inside a large bush was a boy not older than six. He was filthy, mud was in the strands of his long brown hair, and large ticks that looked like they had been sucking blood from him for a long time were stuck all over his back. The child wore only ripped shorts and a rope for a belt.

"Hurry up!" the boy whispered. "It'll be here any minute!"

Arlo could feel the monster closing in, and dove into the brush. Just as he rolled onto his belly to peer outside, eight massive hoofs covered in blood arrived at the spot he'd been standing. Arlo's heart was pounding. He couldn't see the creature's body or face, but he could hear its sounds—an airy, half-spoken human cursing mixed with the grunting and snarling of an angry dog.

"Where arrrrr yoooou? Grrrrr . . . Blooood . . ."

The monster put its large nose to the ground and sniffed. Arlo backed away, afraid the beast would get his scent and come crashing through the trees to take him. He could hear the creature smelling the ground close to where he was hiding. But it lost Arlo's scent and starting sniffing farther up the trail.

Arlo couldn't contain his curiosity and decided to take a look. Slowly he pushed aside a few branches and peered out. What he saw made him jump, and he slapped his hand over his mouth to stop himself from screaming. The creature's face was grotesquely wide, like someone had grabbed both sides of its face and stretched it like taffy. It had four eyes —two on either side of its head and two others sitting atop its forehead. Its mouth was so enormous that the beast couldn't close it, dripping thick saliva everywhere it went. Its skin was green but changed color, alternating from blue to green, then white.

"Wheeere . . . aaare . . . grrrrrr . . ." the creature growled as it sniffed the trail. In frustration, it thrust its head against a tree, sending leaves falling. But still, the monster couldn't find Arlo's hiding spot.

It began searching more frantically. As it moved closer, Arlo's whole body started itching—he could see that the monster's skin wasn't changing colors. Instead, the pores of its skin were breathing, opening to reveal tiny sharp teeth and then snapping shut, pushing a green slimy goo onto the creature's face.

Arlo trembled with fear. Unable to take his eyes off the creature only a few feet away from his hiding spot, he backed away and sat silently, waiting for the monster to burst through and kill him.

Once again, it picked up Arlo's scent and lost it. After releasing several growls and curse words, the creature ripped through the trees and galloped away.

The child stood and looked through the bushes.

"It's gone for now. Come on, let's get out of here before it picks up our scent."

Arlo followed the boy through the forest until they arrived at another trail. The two continued walking until they stopped at the bottom of a hill. The boy picked up a large stick and tossed it into the bushes closest to Arlo. A loud snap rang out, and a large metal bear trap sprung out of the bushes and snapped the stick in half.

"Shit!" exclaimed Arlo. "How'd you know that was there?"

The child walked past Arlo and started climbing the hill.

"Stay close to me now. There are booby traps everywhere, and you will surely die if you don't step as I do."

The two walked on for a few more minutes until the forest thinned, revealing an enormous yellow moon cast against a partially cloudy sky.

"Wow," said Arlo. "What a beautiful moon."

The boy mumbled something under his breath in a deep voice that Arlo didn't understand.

"What did you say?" he asked, trying to see the boy's face. The child looked away, cleared his throat, and pointed to a dip in the path far ahead of them.

"Up ahead. That thing can't reach us beyond that point."

Arlo cast a suspicious glance at the child and continued following him. He knew the boy said something different but wasn't sure what. It sounded like the child said, "He eats the souls."

After walking around a steep mound of soil, a cabin sitting on a hill came into view.

The ominous structure looked old and battered in the moonlight, like it had been there for many years. Although the land it was built upon seemed flat, the house tilted toward the edge of the hill and seemed like it would fall at any moment.

Arlo shuddered at what he saw next: an old rotten wooden fence surrounding a grassless front yard with piles of wet red clay that resembled freshly dug cemetery plots.

Feeling nervous, Arlo started asking questions.

"Who's here?"

"Me and my family."

Arlo saw a dim light shining inside the cabin, but there was no movement.

"You and your family? It seems quiet. Where are they?"

"Everyone's out right now."

"You mean they left you here alone? With that thing running around the forest?"

"I'm not afraid."

The boy pulled open the front gate, and Arlo's knees grew weak; the creaky gate was so loud that it made a group of blackbirds flutter out of the dark forest and land on the dilapidated roof.

Arlo watched as the shoeless boy sloshed through the mud to the porch and grabbed the door handle.

"Are you coming in or what?" the boy asked.

"Hey!" Arlo whispered. "Maybe we should wait until your family comes back."

The little boy released the handle and sat down on the stairs. Eventually, Arlo waded through the muddy yard and sat beside him.

"How long have you lived here?" asked Arlo, nervously trying to make small talk. The boy ignored him and stared straight ahead.

"Does that monster come around here?" asked Arlo.

Finally, the boy spoke.

"He likes you, you know."

"Who? The monster?"

"You know who."

"I don't get it. Why is it chasing—"

Before Arlo could complete his sentence, the boy spoke in another voice, one much deeper and more sinister.

"The time of the beast has almost passed, and he seeks a new vessel."

Startled by the child's sudden transformation, Arlo started trembling. The boy's eyes became beady and bloodshot, and his thin lips curled against his teeth in a scowl. Although he wasn't close to him, Arlo began feeling heat radiating from the boy's body. A brief contemptuous look flickered in the boy's eyes—a look so cold that it made Arlo whisper the word "God" under his breath.

Sensing something much worse would happen if he appeared afraid of the child, Arlo tried pretending he didn't notice the change in the boy. He concentrated and spoke in a calm, even voice.

"A new vessel?"

Suddenly the boy's voice returned to its normal soft-spoken tone, and all the evil melted away.

"You're nice. I think he likes you because you're different than the others."

"Others?"

Once again, the demonic voice exploded out of the child, startling Arlo so much that he registered a visible jump.

"Don't be so fucking stupid! You know what we mean! You all belong to him! All of your souls will burn in his glory!"

Arlo slowly raised himself from the porch and began moving toward the gate.

"Hey, where are you going?" asked the boy as if nothing had happened. He rose from the porch and followed Arlo.

"There's no need for you to be afraid because he likes you."

"You keep saying *he*. Who is *he*?"

"You know."

"No, I don't."

"You will submit! We will have what is ours!"

Arlo wanted to run from the yard and take his chances in the forest. Something about the child's voices terrified him. It was more than the voices. The evil that appeared on the boy's face when he spoke made Arlo afraid for more than just his physical safety. The existence of both good and evil within the same child made Arlo fear for his soul.

"Look, it's obvious that your parents aren't coming any time soon, so I'll just be leaving now."

Suddenly the boy started laughing hysterically.

"You think he wants to hurt you? Is that it?"

"I . . . I don't know what to think."

Suddenly the boy's expression turned serious, and he stopped laughing. His eyes filled with tears, and he started looking all around.

"What is it?" asked Arlo.

The boy walked closer to Arlo, rubbing his arms nervously.

"Please, don't go," he whispered, terrified. "Daddy does things to me—he hurts me."

Arlo stopped walking and stared at the boy. The child's black eyes were cold and glossy, like spotting an iceberg in the freezing ocean on a foggy night. Arlo saw fear in those eyes, and he could see horrible memories replaying—traumatic events that pulled the child away from the muddy lawn and transported him to a cage where he remembered all the pain.

"How?"

"You know."

"Why don't you run away?"

"I can't because he'll find me."

Suddenly the boy ran to Arlo and threw his arms around his waist. Arlo winced in discomfort; the child's body was as cold as a block of ice.

"Are your parents mean like mine?"

Arlo didn't know how to respond to the question, so he remained quiet.

"Parents are supposed to protect and love us, aren't they? Do your parents love you?"

Suddenly the cabin door swung open, and the boy cried out in surprise. A towering dark shadow stood in the doorway, its face hidden from view. The shadow didn't speak. Instead, it stood there holding the door handle, watching the two boys standing in the muddy yard.

"It's Daddy," the boy whispered in a terrified voice. He let go of Arlo's waist and started sloshing through the mud toward the shadow. When the child was halfway through the yard, he ran back to Arlo and placed his cold hand on Arlo's stomach.

"He'll be hungry soon. Feed him, or he'll come out."

The boy turned back, ran up the stairs, and into the house. The shadow lingered in the open doorway, watching Arlo. Slowly, it closed the door.

Arlo was about to run out of the yard when horrible sounds began pouring from the cabin.

"Daddy, please!"

Arlo heard the muffled words of an adult man yelling at the boy, and the child screamed.

"I didn't mean to do it! I promise I'll be a good boy!"

Suddenly the sounds of slaps and punches rang out. Arlo could hear the boy crying.

"Please, Daddy! No more!"

But the sounds of abuse continued, drawing Arlo toward the house.

Suddenly Arlo heard the voice that frightened him most—the boy's demonic personality screamed out.

"No! I said get your fucking hands off me, son of a bitch!"

Something crashed against the front door so hard that the house shook.

"We have had enough of your shit! Come here!"

There was scuffling and more smashing. Finally, Arlo heard a man's voice he'd never heard before.

"Get back! Don't you come near me!"

The demonic voice was laughing now.

"We will taste your fear, you worthless piece of shit! Come here!"

Arlo heard the man scream as the sounds of ripping flesh and cracking bones came from the house. The boy laughed in that possessed voice, enjoying the man's cries of agony.

"We will show you how it feels! We want you to feel what we felt!"

Finally, the man's screaming ceased, and everything was silent. Arlo was about to run out of the yard when he heard a body being dragged across the cabin floor. Suddenly the demonic child spoke again.

"Death will not free you! Come back to us! We have so much hell to show you!"

The child growled several times, and then the house began trembling. Soon the man's voice rang out in pain once more.

"AAAAAAAAHHHHH! Dear God! Help me!"

The child was laughing now, grunting as he seemed to have a hold of the man.

"No one will save your soul! It's ours!"

Suddenly the intensity of the man's screams changed.

"NO! PLEASE! LET GO!"

There was a tearing sound, and the man released a throaty whimper and then fell silent. The ripping of flesh continued, making Arlo cover his mouth in horror. Next, Arlo heard the boy biting and chewing.

"We will taste your fear," the boy growled, gulping greedily.

Although he'd never seen the man's face, the gory sounds fueled Arlo's imagination so horribly that he became nauseous. He imagined the child down on his hands and knees, biting into a bloody corpse like a wild animal, torn flesh hanging from his jowls as he swallowed chunks of his victim.

Arlo backed away from the house and tripped, landing on his back in the mud. After slipping several times, Arlo finally climbed to his feet and reached out to open the gate. Just as he did, a tremendous burning pain shot through his stomach. He lurched forward, hanging on to the fence to prevent himself form falling back to the ground again, but the pain struck him again, filling his mouth with blood.

"Somebody! Help!" Arlo screamed, doubling over in pain.

The pain struck him once more, and this time it was so powerful that he felt the skin of his stomach push out. When he reached down to grab his stomach, he was terrified—he felt something wriggling in his intestines. Arlo ripped open his shirt and watched as the outline of the creature's face appeared and disappeared.

Afraid and bleeding profusely from his mouth, Arlo searched the ground for something with which to kill the creature. He could feel the monster's growls vibrating from his chest to his throat.

"I've got to get this out of me," he cried, falling to his knees.

Suddenly Arlo's stomach exploded, sending blood and black liquid spraying into his face. A long, two-headed, wormlike creature with sharp silver teeth shrieked, thrashing back and forth in his stomach, spraying Arlo's blood all over the yard. He grabbed the monster and pulled it out of his body as the worm screamed, snapping at his face. Arlo threw the worm toward the house and was terrified when it landed on the ground, stood on its tail, growled at him once more, and then burrowed into the mud.

Arlo picked himself up, his insides dangling in the filth, and stumbled to the gate. As he tried to walk out, he felt something on his ankle. He turned to see the yard covered in hundreds of the two-headed worms, all slinking through the mud toward him. Arlo tried to run, but several creatures wrapped themselves around his ankles and sunk their teeth into his skin.

"AAAAAAAHHHH! LET GO OF ME! SOMEONE! HELP!" Arlo screamed.

But soon, they were all atop him, biting into his skin and pulling him beneath the mud. Arlo grabbed handfuls of soil to try to keep himself afloat, but there were too many of the monsters. When he reached out, a beast opened its silver-toothed mouth and bit off Arlo's hand.

"He-help . . . Please," cried Arlo. But soon, he was unable to say anything, his voice stolen by the sudden rush of several of the creatures into the opening in his stomach.

As he sank into the mud, Arlo looked up at the house and saw the child standing in the doorway, covered in blood and holding a human head. He pointed at Arlo as he struggled, enjoying seeing Arlo being eaten alive.

"Are you afraid of them?" he asked in his normal voice. "They love you!"

After watching for a few seconds, the boy looked down and saw something on the porch. He threw the head into the yard, and it landed with a sickening splash atop a pile of slithering worms directly in front of Arlo's face.

The boy bent down to pick up the item that caught his attention—the man's intestines. He stuffed the entrails into his mouth and almost swallowed them whole.

Suddenly he yelled at Arlo in his demonic voice.

"We are almost out of time! You will join us, or we shall all feast on your soul!"

Just as Arlo's eyes disappeared beneath the mud, the boy turned around and walked back into the house.

31

The Dinner Party

When Arlo woke up, he was lying on the sofa in the TV room. He knew it was late because the channel he usually watched was showing infomercials.

"Shit," Arlo complained, squinting at the television screen. "Something must be wrong with the TV—the color's off."

Arlo grabbed the remote and turned off the TV. As he sat in darkness, he realized that something was different. Arlo could see everything in the room without turning on the light. He walked over to the window and looked outside; the night seemed no darker than daylight, and Arlo saw every blade of grass as clearly as if the sun was shining.

Arlo watched as a fox emerged from the forest and walked to the yard's edge. As if sensing that Arlo was watching it, the animal paused, looked up at him, and then walked onto the lawn. Suddenly there was a loud click, and the security lights illuminated the yard. The brightness of the security lights flooded the TV room, drenching Arlo in their brilliance and causing him to stumble backward. As he shaded his eyes, he tripped over the coffee table and fell hard on his face.

"Shit," he mumbled, rubbing his head.

Suddenly Arlo's body stiffened, and he lifted his head.

"What *is* that?" he asked, rising to his feet. Something smelled delicious.

"Roasted pork and pineapple?" he asked, breathing deeply. Suddenly Arlo's stomach growled loudly, and he touched his belly. He realized then that he hadn't eaten anything for two days.

Arlo walked out of the room and downstairs to the kitchen. There was a plate of empanadas on the counter that his mother had left out for him. Without warming the food in the microwave, Arlo quickly tossed aside the plastic cover, grabbed a handful of food, and shoved it into his mouth. Arlo's nostrils began burning, and his eyes filled with water. Gagging and coughing, he spat the food into the sink.

"What the fuck?!" he asked.

The food tasted like vinegar. Arlo lifted the remaining plate of food and smelled it—the enchiladas smelled as they always did. Frustrated, Arlo slung the food onto the counter and used his fingernails to scratch the residue from his tongue—the food was still burning his nose, causing it to run. Arlo wiped his nose with the back of his hand and went to the refrigerator. He opened it, grabbed a carton of orange juice, and drank from the carton. This time the stinging sensation in his nose was so intense that vomit shot from his mouth. Arlo dropped the juice carton on the floor and fell back, gasping for air. He shot to the kitchen sink, turned on the faucet, and splashed water into his mouth.

"What the hell is happening to me?" he asked, the burning of the orange juice subsiding. After a few seconds, the burning feeling was gone. Arlo was about to return to his room when the aroma of food entered his nose again, making his stomach growl loudly.

"Where is that smell coming from?" he asked, sniffing the air.

Arlo was about to walk back to his room when he smelled the food again—this time much more intense. It seemed to be coming from the living room. Arlo continued sniffing the air as he walked, his stomach growling louder as the delicious scent took over his senses. Soon his shirt was wet with drool, and he opened his mouth to taste the smell. Arlo had never wanted something so much in his life; his hands trembled, and his stomach began cramping out of desire—he had to taste it.

As soon as he arrived in the living room, Arlo froze—his father was asleep on the sofa. The aroma seemed to be coming from him! Arlo tried to look away but couldn't. The skin on his father's face glistened in the darkness like the most delicious cut of meat he'd ever seen. Arlo fantasized about how the meat tasted, how it would be when his father's sweet juices exploded in his mouth as Arlo ripped apart the flesh with his teeth. He started thinking about which parts of his body were most meaty.

Arlo could smell Jaime's insides with every snore from his father's mouth, pushing a sweet, nutty odor into Arlo's face. He quickly looked back at the staircase to see if his mother was nearby—she wasn't. Arlo moved closer to his father, the aroma growing stronger. He began thinking about various ways to consume the man without leaving a mess.

"If I do it quickly, I can clean up before Mom gets up," he whispered. "Nobody will know."

Arlo moved closer, licking his lips as saliva poured from his mouth like water. He wanted to eat him—no, he *had* to eat him.

Just as Arlo reached out to grab his father, Jaime suddenly sat up and screamed.

"AAAAAAAHHHH!" yelled Jaime, looking around the dark room.

The scream startled Arlo, and he stumbled back, seemingly lost and confused. Jaime reached over and switched on the lamp.

"Jesus Christ!" he said, rubbing his eyes.

He soon noticed Arlo standing a few feet away.

"Arlo. What are you doing here? Did I wake you?"

Arlo heard footsteps running down the stairs, and his mother stood behind him.

"What is it? What's all the yelling?" she asked, her face covered in white cream.

Arlo stumbled for words, and then spoke.

"I . . . I heard Dad yelling in his sleep."

Claire looked from her son's face to her husband's.

"Jesus, Jaime. You're keeping everyone awake with that alcohol. Go to bed."

Arlo turned and sped away from his parents. The scent had multiplied since his mother entered the room, and he didn't know how much longer he could keep control of himself—he wanted to eat them both.

32

Evasion

Arlo sat on the edge of his bed, trying to calm himself. He kept telling himself he'd experienced the cannibalistic episode through sleep-walking, that maybe he'd seen something on TV that filtered into his dreams. But Arlo knew the truth—he wanted to taste his parents' flesh more than anything, and nothing would change that. The delicious aroma of his parents' meat moved his soul. Though Arlo tried lying to himself about his undying love for his parents, nothing was more significant than the hunger tearing him apart from the inside, the urge to consume their bodies and drink their sweet blood.

"Shit!" Arlo cursed. "This can't be real!"

Arlo finally got up and went into the bathroom, searching for any-thing to take his mind off the hunger. After a few seconds, he grabbed his toothbrush, covered it in toothpaste, and shoved it in his mouth. A burning ammonia smell shot pain into the back of his brain, caus-ing him to drop the toothbrush and spit out the vile paste. He put his mouth to the water faucet and turned it on full blast—eventually diminishing the burning in his nose. After a few seconds, he tried smell-ing the air—the smell of his parents' bodies was more pungent.

"I need to get out of here," whispered Arlo.

He went to the closet, grabbed his jacket, and was about to exit when the telephone rang. Arlo recognized the phone number. It was Manuel.

"Hello? Mani?"

Manuel didn't respond. Instead, Arlo heard him sniffing and breathing heavily.

"Mani? Are you crying? What's going on?"

Finally, Manuel responded.

"Arlo! You gotta come quick!" he whispered.

"What is it? Did you find something?"

"I . . . I did something horrible. Oh my God! What kind of a son . . ."

Manuel's sobs became audible. Suddenly he stopped crying.

"Wait! Something's wrong!"

Manuel placed the receiver down, and Arlo began to panic.

"Mani! Mani! You there?"

After a few moments, Manuel picked up the phone.

"Jesus, Arlo! They're everywhere! What am I going to do? I can't get out!"

"Who's there?"

"The monster dogs and the kids have the house surrounded!"

"Stay there, Mani! I'm coming!"

Arlo hung up the phone and ran to his bedroom window. He opened the blinds to see if the evil children surrounded his home, but when he looked outside, there was nothing but an empty yard.

Arlo ran out of his room and was about to run down the stairs when he stopped a few steps beyond his parents' bedroom door. The smell pouring out of their room was so intoxicating that his mind became a scrambled mess. Visions of biting into their flesh made saliva flow from his mouth anew. His nose began running, and his hands trembled. He could feel the hunger pushing him toward their room.

And then something inside Arlo settled.

Somehow he was able to push the wicked thoughts out of his mind and refocus. Slowly, one foot after the other, Arlo backed away from his parents' room and turned toward the stairway. After wiping his nose and mouth, he bounded down the stairs and burst out of the front door. Once in the street, Arlo didn't see the lights in his house turn on. He could only think of one thing—his friend.

Arlo sprinted past every house on his street until Manuel's house came into view. Fearing he'd be spotted, Arlo ran into some bushes at the side of the house and waited. Soon he saw them—two of the enormous demon dogs walked across Manuel's front yard with the two boys walking behind them. A dozen ghost children emerged from the backyard and followed the others, seemingly patrolling the property.

Arlo saw his chance. He grabbed a stone from the ground and hurled it into Manuel's neighbor's window on the opposite side of the street. The crash was loud, and the lights inside several houses came on. The children immediately ran toward the sound. As soon as the dogs and children were out of sight, Arlo entered the house and ran upstairs.

"Mani!" he whispered as he climbed the stairs. "Where are you? It's me, Arlo!"

Arlo ran down the hallway toward his friend's room and stopped. Manuel was on his knees in front of the bathroom, covered in blood and gnawing on a human skeleton.

"Mani!" Arlo whispered, tiptoeing closer. "Hey, Mani! It's me, Arlo."

Manuel looked up from the corpse and growled at Arlo, blood covering his face, chunks of flesh hanging from his mouth.

"Take it easy, Mani! It's me!"

Suddenly Manuel's eyes softened, and he dropped the bones to the floor.

"Arlo? Is it really you?"

Arlo moved closer to his friend.

"Yeah, dude. It's me."

Manuel's eyes filled with tears, and he covered his face with his bloody hands and began sobbing.

"I don't know what's wrong with me," he cried. "Why is this happening?"

Arlo rubbed his friend's shoulders to console him.

"Come on. Let's get out of here."

Manuel looked up at Arlo, tears streaming down his face.

"I . . . I don't know why this is happening. The hunger . . . My daddy. Oh my God, what am I going to do?"

"Where's your mom and your sister?"

Manuel ignored the question.

"I was just so hungry. I tried to eat dinner, but the food burned."

Arlo looked around nervously. Manuel's sobbing was sure to get the attention of the dogs. They had to leave.

"Mani, let's get out of here."

"What am I going to tell my mom when she comes home? What am I going to say to Maria? I killed our father!"

Arlo knelt beside Manuel and whispered in his ear.

"This wasn't your fault, Mani. I don't blame you."

"You don't?"

"No, I don't. But those monsters will come in and take us if we stay here too long."

"Where will we go? They're everywhere."

"We're going to the only place we can go—to John's house."

Manuel's face turned serious, and he wiped his tears away.

"His house? Did you find a way to stop him?"

"He destroyed our families, so let's destroy his home."

"Are you sure that'll work? I mean, he's so powerful."

Arlo smiled and slapped his friend on the head, then stood up.

"It's like you said, Mani. I'm not going out without a fight. You coming?"

Slowly Manuel rose to his feet.

"That son of a bitch made me kill my father. Hell, yeah, I'm going to fight."

"Do you know where the house is?"

"Yeah. I downloaded the location to my cellphone."

"Good. Let's go."

The boys ran down the stairs and looked out the living room window. The creatures were back and patrolling Manuel's property while some of the ghostly children entered and exited the house across the street.

"I don't get it. Those bastards know where I am and could come in to kill me anytime. Why are they just walking around like zombies?" whispered Manuel.

"My guess? They're waiting on John's instructions."

The boys grew silent as an enormous devil dog walked in front of the window. It paused, lifted its head to smell the air, and then continued walking to the corner of the house.

"Where did you park your scooter?"

"In the garage. We'd never be able to get it started before those dogs came running. It's too noisy, and they'd hear us for sure."

"Maybe. But what if I had a distraction?"

"A distraction?"

"What if I ran out and drew them away from the house long enough for you to start the bike and get away?"

"Are you crazy? Those dog things would chase you down."

"Sure, if they found me. But I think I know how to throw those dogs off our trail."

"How?"

"They're dogs, right? And last I checked, all dogs like bones."

"I don't like where you're going with this, Arlo. I couldn't do that. Please don't make me go back there."

"Well, what choice do we have? We go upstairs, get your dad's bones, and toss them to draw the dogs away from the house. You get away, and we'll meet up after we clear the dogs."

"And what about the kids?"

"We just have to outrun them. Those zombie kids are only following John's orders. Even your little sister could outrun them. Just give me enough time to go upstairs to get the bones, and I'll distract them while you start the motorcycle."

"And where will we meet up?"

"Down the street at the gas station."

"That's kind of far, Arlo. Are you sure you're going to make it?"

"Don't worry about me. I'll be fine."

Arlo ran upstairs to the pile of bones. When he saw the mush on the floor, he realized that collecting the bones would be messier than he'd thought. Arlo entered Manuel's bedroom, grabbed his gym bag, and returned to the corpse. As he knelt to pick up the bones, he saw Manuel's father's severed head staring at him from the bathroom floor. Arlo felt a sadness in his chest. Although Manuel told him of his father's abuse, Arlo did have a few fond memories of the man—the time he picked them both up from the bus stop in a thunderstorm to take them to get burgers, and another time when he took them to a baseball game.

Arlo shook the memories out of his head and grabbed the two femur bones from the floor. When he held them, he was surprised at how deep Manuel's teeth had penetrated, dozens of deep indentations with blood oozing from the cracks.

Once he got the bones into the bag, he ran downstairs and saw Manuel peeping out the window.

"Okay, I got them," said Arlo. "You ready?"

Manuel's eyes filled with tears, and he turned away.

"Please, Arlo. Let's get this over with. The smell . . . I don't have any control. Please get it away from me."

Arlo looked at the bag and quickly jerked it away from Manuel.

"Okay, go ahead and start up the motorcycle. I'm heading out now."

Arlo watched Manuel run into the kitchen and open the door leading to the garage. When he heard the motorcycle's engine, he ran out of the house into the front yard. As soon as he did, two young boys turned around and ran toward him.

"YOOOOOOU . . ."

Arlo didn't panic—he quickly kicked one of the boys in the stomach and slammed the bag of bones into the head of the other, sending them both tumbling to the ground. Suddenly four more teens appeared from the corner of the house and charged at Arlo. Just as they reached him, the garage door opened, and Manuel shot out, speeding across the lawn. The four teens turned around and charged at Manuel, but he was too far ahead.

"Arlo! Get out of there!" yelled Manuel as he sped up the street. Several people heard the noise and opened their doors to look outside.

Suddenly there was a great roar, and two of the monster dogs appeared from the side of the house. One took off running after Manuel while the other charged Arlo, stepping on and crushing two kids as it rushed him. Arlo reached into the bag, grabbed a bone, and hurled it into the trees. The creature instantly went after it, smashing into a large oak tree, causing it to fall over and land on the house.

Arlo took off running up the street. Although the other animal hadn't caught Manuel yet, he could see the monster gaining on him.

"HEY!" yelled Arlo. "I'M OVER HERE!"

The beast heard him, turned around, and charged. Arlo grabbed another bone and hurled it into the trees, making the animal leap after the bone. Just as the first dog emerged from the forest, the other dog smashed into it, and both animals cried out in pain. As they tumbled into the woods, knocking over trees, Arlo punched three other children and sprinted up the street. He cut through several backyards and onto another road until he was sure no one was following. Exhausted and frightened, he broke into a jog on his way to the gas station.

33

Filling Up

"Shit, dude, I thought you didn't make it," said Manuel as Arlo walked over to the motorcycle.

Arlo smiled at his friend while wiping blood on his pants.

"Yeah, I made it. You got your cell phone?"

Manuel tapped his pocket.

"Right here."

"Good. We need to get going before those things find us."

"Yeah, but what are we going to do? We don't have anything to kill John."

Arlo smiled and walked over to the dumpster sitting at the corner of the gas station. He opened the metal doors and dug around until he found a plastic container.

"You got any cash on you?" he asked, walking over to the gas pump.

"No, but I've got my cash app. What's up?"

Arlo nodded toward the building.

"Fill 'er up."

Manuel disappeared inside the station while Arlo started filling the plastic container with gas, keeping an eye out for the hell spawn. Seconds later, Manuel emerged.

"Dude, I picked up a book of matches too, but now we have to go. The attendant looked at all the blood on my clothes and dialed the cops."

Arlo finished filling the container, paid for the gas with his cash app, and climbed on Manuel's motorcycle.

"I'll drive, and you tell me where we're going."

Manuel pulled up the location on his cell phone, and the two boys drove off into the night.

34

Bigger Than Words

"It's in there."

Arlo slowed the motorcycle and pulled over to the side of the highway.

"There?" he asked, pointing to a dusty road on the other side of a metal gate.

"Yeah."

"Do you know how far in we have to go?"

"You're kidding, right? I have a cell phone, not a hundred-thousand-dollar global positioning system from the U.S. Government. I only looked up Black Hills Forest, and I guess this is the entrance everyone uses."

"So that house could be anywhere."

"Yep."

Arlo climbed off the motorcycle and walked over to the metal barrier. He saw an old wooden structure at the end of the road, but beyond that was nothing but trees.

"That's the security checkpoint over there."

"Security? Out here? That's nothing but a place for those idiots to try to collect an entrance fee for doing nothing."

Arlo climbed over the metal gate and placed the gas container on the ground.

"Hey, Mani, did any of your dreams take place in a forest?"

"Some of them, but it's all a blur. I can't remember anything about those dreams beyond being scared. Jesus! The things that happened to me in those nightmares were terrible, and I'm afraid of just thinking about them. He made me do things like—"

Arlo cut Manuel off.

"Have you ever visited this place?" he asked, intentionally interrupting Manuel. "I haven't, but I heard it's pretty cool."

Arlo wanted both their minds sharp—he didn't need Manuel remembering that he killed his father.

"You'll be our navigation because I can't remember shit."

"We might as well get going," he said, taking the container of gasoline from Manuel.

Manuel stared at him incredulously.

"Are you serious? It's pitch black, and this forest is huge. How are we going to find the way to the house?"

"We have to try, don't we? What other choice do we have?"

Manuel parked his bike against the metal barrier and climbed over behind Arlo.

"I can't wait to kill that son of a bitch!" he growled.

"Me, too, Mani," replied Arlo. "Me, too."

35

Blind Sight

Arlo and Manuel tried their best to navigate the forest as the night wore on. Whenever something looked familiar, Arlo told Manuel, and they explored it. But after a while, the forest became a world with two confusing viewpoints—a place filled with everything that seemed recognizable and a hostile alien landscape. It didn't take long before Arlo realized they were lost.

After stumbling through the woods for hours, the two boys came upon a clearing of soft grass surrounded by towering trees. Feeling exhausted and frustrated, they sat down to catch their breath.

"How much longer do you want to search?" asked Manuel.

Arlo looked around the forest to see if he saw anything familiar. Realizing he didn't, he sighed.

"As long as it takes."

Manuel laid on the grass and closed his eyes.

"Just give me a few minutes to catch my breath."

As Manuel nodded off, Arlo continued looking around the forest for anything that seemed familiar. Although it was dark, his vision was just as crisp as earlier, and the nocturnal life in the woods revealed itself to him; just a few feet away from where he sat, Arlo saw a giant black snake dislocating its jaw to swallow a toad. To his right, he saw a line of ants dragging the carcass of a bird across the grass.

"Like us, I suppose," Arlo said, and chuckled. He, too, felt like an empty version of himself being dragged through the forest by something that wanted to eat his soul. Feeling sorry for the bird, Arlo picked up a stick and tossed it at the ants to break up their victorious march.

Taking a bit of satisfaction from scattering the army of ants, Arlo continued looking around. Nothing seemed familiar. He wondered if their attempt at stopping John was just the silly fantasies of two immature kids with overactive imaginations. When Arlo thought about it, the John situation seemed like something out of a comic book. Sure, he'd seen Isadora transform from someone he thought about having a relationship with to a monster who wanted to eat his face off, but no one else saw the girl—not even Manuel. And his fear of John? It was mostly in his head—nightmarish recollections of a lonely teenager who was fond of poetry.

Arlo laid on the grass and looked up into the trees. The problems in his life felt silly and clumsy, like trying to stuff a basketball into a microwave.

Suddenly Arlo saw movement in his peripheral—something small and white appeared and disappeared amongst the trees. Arlo's imagination started running wild; maybe one of the zombie kids followed them, or perhaps it was Isadora coming to kill and eat him.

Slowly Arlo scratched at his pants leg and tilted his head to see what was watching them. His heart almost stopped beating—the boy from his nightmare was staring at him.

Arlo stayed still and was afraid to scream. He lowered his eyes to the ground and kept them there, afraid to make direct eye contact with the demon. Arlo tried to eliminate his fear by concentrating; he held his breath and tried pushing the anxiety toward the tips of his toes. But the fright of knowing what was watching him from the shadows was too great, too real. His fear quickly manifested and took control of his body; both Arlo's legs began bouncing uncontrollably, and he started wheezing. Sensing he was losing it, Arlo quickly looked to Manuel for help.

But the boy's loud snoring was the only response Manuel provided, leaving Arlo alone with an audience of evil intent.

Finally, Arlo summoned the courage to look directly at the demon. Slowly he raised his head and stared at the monster—the boy looked scarier than the child in Arlo's nightmare; his skin was pale with a bluish tinge, tiny veins pulsating in his face. The demon kept shifting his position: he'd lean out behind the tree to scare Arlo, then move back behind the tree, his meatless arms and boney fingers moving along the tree trunk, like giant spiders, his wide dark blue eyes watching to see Arlo's reaction. He sneered at Arlo, an angry yet taunting display meant to simultaenously frighten him and make a mockery of him. Arlo looked away the first time, and the monster seemed to celebrate the accomplishment. But the second time the demon sneered, Arlo held firm and stared back. He could see the evil burning beneath the surface of the monster and knew it was searching for the slightest display of weakness.

Finally, furious that his appearance didn't inflict the same fear in Arlo's eyes the second time, the monster curled its chapped lips against its black teeth, released a terrifying growl, and ran into the trees.

Arlo snatched the can of gas from the ground and kicked Manuel's foot to wake him.

"Mani! Let's go!"

By the time Manuel woke up, Arlo was pushing through the bushes. He had to keep up with the demon if they had any hope of finding John's house.

"Arlo!" yelled Manuel from behind. "Slow down!"

Arlo ran through a group of bushes and stopped; he'd lost the boy. Eventually, Manuel ran up behind him, out of breath.

"What's going on? Why are you running?"

"I saw him."

"Who?"

"The boy in my dreams."

"In your dreams? What do you mean?"

Suddenly Arlo saw blue skin move past the bushes ahead of him, and he took off running again. Gasoline splashed on his clothes, but he didn't care. If the boy got away, they might be unable to find their way to John's house.

Arlo jumped over a large log and then splashed across a small river while Manuel struggled to keep up. Eventually, they arrived at the bottom of a hill, and Arlo stopped; he didn't need to follow the demon anymore because he recognized everything from his dream.

"Okay, Mani. Here is where things get tricky. Walk where I walk and step where I step. John booby-trapped the forest."

"Booby-trapped?! Who the hell is this guy, MacGyver or something?"

"Mind where you step. If either of us gets hurt, we're screwed."

Suddenly the child darted across the path in front of the two boys, and Manuel screamed.

"Shit! Did you see that?"

"Don't worry about him. I know where we're going now."

The boys continued walking until the forest opened to a winding road at the base of a large hill. Occasionally Arlo would lose sight of the child, but then the boy would reappear and try to get them to walk in a different direction. But Arlo knew better; the child was trying to lure them into a trap. Eventually, the demon boy disappeared, and the boys walked up the winding road without interruption until the old house on the hill came into sight.

"Jesus. We have to go in there?" asked Manuel.

Arlo didn't respond because he couldn't take his eyes off the house. It was just as it had been in his nightmare—including the muddy holes that looked like burial plots. Arlo remembered how the worms had pulled him beneath the mud, wriggling themselves through his ribcage and eating his insides. He remembered the demon child's smile as the creatures pulled him under, the euphoric look on the boy's face as he took pleasure in seeing the life fading from Arlo's eyes.

Now Arlo was here again. Except this time, the morbid place teased his senses; he could smell the rot in the air and hear the creaking of the old house as the biting wind pushed it, causing it to dangle on the edge of the hill, ready to fall at any moment. Beyond the boys staring at the house, nothing living stirred—no owls, no birds, no life—just cold evil and the pounding hearts of two terrified children.

Arlo was about to walk into the front yard when a blue streak shot past him and went around the house. This time instead of ignoring the child, Arlo chased him.

"Hey, Arlo!" yelled Manuel. "Wait up! Don't leave me!"

As soon as Arlo arrived at the backyard, he stopped. The evil boy stood at the far end of the backyard, next to an old wooden outhouse. He smiled at Arlo with his tiny black teeth and darted behind the structure. As soon as he did, Manuel arrived.

"Dude! You have to stop leaving me! That isn't cool."

Arlo ignored his best friend's complaining and pointed to the outhouse.

"There! He ran behind that thing."

Arlo started walking to the outhouse while Manuel stood hesitant to follow.

"Arlo! Are you sure about following him?"

Arlo paused and turned to Manuel.

"Look, Mani. Stop behaving like a scared pussy. At first I didn't want to follow him because it might be a trap. But now we're all twisted around and lost. What other choice do we have? Have you seen anyone else this deep in the woods? That little bastard's leading us to John, and killing John is the only way all this ends. You coming or not?"

Manuel looked around nervously before finally deciding to follow Arlo.

"Let's hurry up and get this over with. This place creeps me out," whispered Manuel.

"Cool with me," replied Arlo.

When the boys looked behind the outhouse, they expected to find the ghost boy waiting to attack them. Instead, what they found were overgrown weeds.

"I don't get it," whispered Manuel, confused. "Didn't he come back here?"

"Yeah. I saw him," replied Arlo.

Arlo kicked aside the weeds, searching for the boy. Suddenly his foot struck a metal object.

"What is it?" asked Manuel.

Arlo pushed aside the weeds until he could see the object clearly—a rusty metal door covering a hole in the ground. Arlo pulled on the door's handle but couldn't lift it.

"Give me a hand, Mani."

"What, you can't open it? How'd that little boy get in there?"

Both boys grabbed the handle and pulled until they could slide the door aside. As soon as they did, a rank odor shot out in a cloud of smoke.

"My God! It smells like shit down there," exclaimed Mani. But Arlo recognized the smell; it was the same in the museum and his bedroom.

"You got those matches from the gas station?"

Manuel dug into his pockets, pulled out the matches, and passed them to Arlo. Arlo struck a match and held it down into the hole—he couldn't see anything, so he lowered himself farther.

"You see anything?" asked Manuel.

"Nah, nothing," said Arlo, squinting into the darkness. "Hold onto my belt."

Manuel grabbed Arlo's belt and lowered Arlo a little farther.

"I see a ladder."

"How far down does it go?"

"I don't know. Try lowering me a little bit more."

"I'm trying, dude, but you're heavy!"

"Hurry up before the match goes out."

Arlo's eyes followed the ladder down as far as he could see, but eventually, it disappeared into the darkness. Finally, the fire reached Arlo's fingertips and burned him.

"Ow!" he screamed and dropped the match.

"What is it?"

"The match went out."

"Shit. Well, that's that, I suppose."

Arlo was frustrated. His vision was so sharp in the forest, and now he couldn't see five feet in front of his face.

"Pull me up, Mani."

Suddenly a decaying face with dead eyes burst from the shadows and grabbed Arlo.

"YOOOOOOU!"

"HOLY SHIT!" yelled Arlo, trying to cover his face. "PULL ME UP! PULL ME UP!"

But the demon was strong and held Arlo tight in its grasp. The monster pulled close to Arlo's face and opened its mouth.

"YOOOOOOOU!"

Arlo could smell the corpse's rotting flesh and tried pushing it away. But soon, dozens of cold dead hands were all around him, clawing at him and scratching his face.

"MANI, PULL ME UP!"

"I CAN'T, ARLO. SOMETHING'S GOT ME! I CAN'T BREAK FREE!"

Arlo tried to raise himself, but something from behind pushed him and sent both him and Manuel falling into darkness.

"ARLOOOOOOO . . ." yelled Manuel.

But Arlo couldn't respond. His descent into blackness left him disoriented. As he tumbled head over heels, he tried to gain his bearings, but everything was a blur. Not sure what death would be like, Arlo closed his eyes and waited for impact.

He thought of all the people he'd never see again. His mother, would never discover the location of his body. There would be no viewing of her son's body, only the cold police report of an unaccounted-for son, which would drive his mother insane. Arlo's father, who Arlo hated an unbelievable amount, would be grateful to be relieved of his responsibilities. Arlo imagined the smile on his father's face as the police told him his son was a missing person. The asshole would smile smugly, taking comfort in knowing his minimal level of responsibility was gone.

Within these thoughts, Arlo waited for death.

But it never came.

There was only silence cloaked in darkness.

Eventually, Arlo opened his eyes. Although he could only see blackness, he knew he was lying on the ground. Arlo quickly rolled onto his stomach and raised himself to his feet.

"Mani, you there?" he asked, his voice echoing.

But there was no response. Arlo began thinking the worst—that his friend hadn't survived the fall and that Manuel's twisted, mangled corpse was in the bottom of the hole. But soon, selfishness washed over Arlo, and he became grateful to survive the fall. Surviving allowed him to relax, but only slightly. A more sinister thought began eating at his brain: what if he couldn't get out? How would he die? Starvation? Injury? Loneliness? Or would the demon boy watch his suffering until Arlo was weak and then come out of the shadows to feast on his carcass? Arlo closed his eyes once more and took in a scared breath. Now an instant death seemed like something he should've hoped to have. Feeling alone and afraid, Arlo called out for his friend again.

"Mani?" he called out again. "Are you okay? You here?"

There was movement at Arlo's ankle.

"Y-yeah, I'm here, dude."

"Mani!"

Arlo was elated. He reached down, grabbed his friend by the arm, and lifted him to his feet.

"Shit, Mani, I thought you were a goner."

"Me, too. Where the hell are we?"

The two boys embraced while straining their eyes to look around.

"I don't know. Inside that hole, I think."

"Why did you scream? Did you see something?"

"I don't want to talk about that now. Let's focus on getting out of here. Can you see anything?"

"No. What about those matches?"

"Oh, yeah, I have the matches in my pocket. Mani, I don't know what I'd do without you."

Arlo fumbled around in his jeans until his finger latched onto the matchbox. Cautiously he struck a match.

Both boys screamed out in horror at what they saw. They were standing in the center of a large room with dead bodies. Some decomposed bodies barely seemed human, and some seemed to have just died. But they were all covered in mud, worms crawling all over them.

Manuel looked at the bodies and instantly vomited while Arlo covered his nose and continued holding the match. He knelt close to the bodies to see the faces; although many wore twisted expressions of torture, none of them were people Arlo recognized.

"Jesus, Arlo. There's so many of them."

"I know."

"But . . . all of these people seem to be *adults*. How do you suppose they got here?"

Arlo ripped the blouse off a female corpse, exposing her gray breast.

"God, Arlo. That's awful," complained Manuel. "Don't touch them!"

Arlo looked around until he found a broken tree branch on the floor. He wrapped the blouse around the stick and used the match to ignite it. As the fire lit up the room, both boys stared in disbelief. Hundreds of bodies were in the room with them; some were missing limbs, while others were missing chunks of flesh as though something had taken bites out of them. Arlo shivered when his eyes fell on the body of an old man; the corpse seemed to be staring directly at Arlo, smiling at him with half his face missing.

"Hey, Arlo. Do you think we're going to die in here?"

The question startled Arlo, and he looked at Manuel and noticed he was crying. Arlo grabbed Manuel's arm and pulled him close.

"We're going to make it out of here, do you hear me? Don't start giving up. That son of a bitch would love that."

Manuel nodded his head in agreement and wiped his face.

"Hey!" he exclaimed, pointing to the far side of the room. "What's that over in the corner?"

Arlo swung the torch over to where Manuel was pointing.

"That looks like our way out. Come on, let's go!"

The boys began making their way through the bodies toward the door. Arlo tried not to step on the corpses but couldn't avoid them. Manuel almost fell, and Arlo grabbed him by the arm.

"Be careful, dude."

"There's just so many of them, like walking on a sponge cake and rocks."

Arlo couldn't disguise his disgust as he moved through the dead people. He knew what Manuel meant—some of the bodies felt soft under his feet like mush, while others' brittle bones cracked under his weight.

Arlo coughed a couple of times, almost dropping the torch.

"You okay?" asked Manuel.

"I'll be alright," replied Arlo.

But he wasn't alright. Arlo thought he'd become immune to the smell of mud, feces, and decaying flesh, but so much death was in the room that the smell began choking him. At that moment, Arlo realized every person who carried the odor—Isadora, the evil twins, the children in the museum—had all been in the room.

As the boys drew closer to the door, Arlo stopped walking and stared.

"What is it?" asked Manuel.

It was the old woman from Arlo's dream propped up against the wall next to the door. Her eyes were gone, and fresh mud poured out of her eye sockets in a steady stream.

"What? She was in your dreams, too?"

"Yeah."

Arlo moved closer to the woman and swung the torch in front of her face.

"Yeah, it's her. But . . ."

"But what?"

"Look at her."

Although the other bodies in the room were dead, Arlo couldn't tell if the old woman from his dreams was alive; she was still plump, and although covered in mud, her brown skin showed no signs of decay.

"She's dead, right?" asked Arlo.

Manuel moved closer to the woman.

"She's got to be. Look at her face. She's missing her eyes, and mud is coming from her face. Who could live through something like that?"

"But that's fresh mud. How is it pouring from her face?"

"I don't know. Maybe her head is close to a faucet or something."

Suddenly the boys heard a sound—a metal can falling on the opposite side of the room.

"What was that?" asked Arlo, spinning around to shine the light into the room behind them.

"Come on, man. Let's get out of here," whispered Manuel.

Arlo was about to leave when he spotted something on that opposite side of the room: two red dots moving back and forth over a pile of bodies. Finally, the object came into full view—it was the demon boy. He lifted one of the corpses from the ground and bit off a chunk of the man's face. The monster opened his mouth wide and hissed at Arlo, his black teeth growing out of his mouth like black knives.

"RUN!" screamed Arlo.

Both boys ran out of the room and into a long, hollow passageway. Arlo looked behind, and his knees almost gave out; all the corpses piled through the doorway after them, pulling and clawing at one another.

Finally, the two boys entered an open room filled with a muddy lake.

"What do we do?" asked Manuel.

Arlo didn't hesitate—he dropped the torch onto the ground, jumped into the mud, and started wading to the other side.

"No fucking way!" complained Manuel, eventually jumping in. "This is so gross!"

Arlo tried not to think of what was in the mud but couldn't help himself. The sludge shooting up his nose and into his mouth tasted as horrible as it smelled. Still, he continued pushing through while Manuel continued complaining.

"I think I'm going to be sick."

"Shut up and get to the other side before they come in after us!"

Arlo was halfway to the other side when the corpses reached the mud. But instead of jumping in to chase the boys, the monsters stayed at the edge of the cesspool, growling.

"I don't get it," complained Arlo. "Why aren't they jumping in after us?"

"Who cares? Let's get out of here!"

Arlo reached the other side of the room and pulled himself out of the sludge. Just as he did, he remembered the matches in his pocket.

"Shit!" he cursed, looking at the dimming torch on the other side of the room. No matter where they went, it would be in complete darkness. Angry at the loss of the matches, Arlo's body began itching. Frantically, he started scratching his body all over. When Manuel arrived, he noticed his friend scratching himself uncontrollably.

"What is it?"

"I don't know, but I'm itching like crazy."

Manuel started scratching, too, and peeled off his clothes. Arlo stopped scratching and stared at his friend in disbelief.

"Oh my God."

Dozens of worms were on Manuel's body—the same translucent monsters Arlo had seen in his dream. They were curled up on Manuel's skin like leeches, trying to burrow into his body.

"AAAAAHHH!" screamed Manuel. "GET THEM OFF! GET THEM OFF!"

Arlo started pulling at the worms on Manuel's skin as quickly as he could; every time he grabbed a worm, the creature released its circular mouth from Manuel's flesh and attempted to bite Arlo's hand before falling to the ground.

"They're falling off easily," explained Arlo, ignoring the parasites tearing at his body.

"I don't give a damn! Just get them off!"

Arlo looked across the room at the growling zombies standing at the edge of the mud; he now understood why they hadn't chased them.

Finally, Arlo pulled the last creature from Manuel's skin.

"Your turn," said Manuel.

Arlo stripped down to his underwear, and he and Manuel began pulling the creatures from his skin. When they finished, both boys looked at one another before opening their underwear and shoving their hands inside. After a few moments of exploring their genitals and buttocks, they smiled.

"Man!"

"I thought for sure they got me!"

With a watchful eye on the menacing monsters on the other side of the room, the boys took a few moments to shake the mud and worms off before putting their clothes on again. At that moment, Arlo noticed the outline of a door on the dark wall.

"Hey! It's a door."

Arlo could tell that whoever made the door never intended for it to be open from the inside; he had to run his fingers along the wall until he found the edges of the door. If it had been dark, there's no way they would've discovered it.

"It's a hidden door."

"Hidden?"

"Yeah."

Arlo looked closer at the wall and felt sick—bloody fingernails were on it.

"This place is a prison meant to keep people from escaping until the worms get inside them."

"People like us."

Manuel moved away from the pile of worms twisting on the floor.

"I've got a feeling this place is much more dangerous than we've seen. Let's get out of here," Manuel said, turning to the door.

Arlo ran his fingers along the edges of the door until he found a spot where he could slide them inside. After struggling for a few seconds, he opened the door, grateful to see a dim light shining from beyond.

"Where do you suppose it leads?" asked Manuel.

"Anywhere but here," replied Arlo.

Feeling No Feelings

The boys ran through the door into another hallway lined with stones. As they moved along the dank corridor, a sinking feeling overcame Arlo, and he didn't want to proceed. No matter what awaited them at the end of the hallway, they wouldn't make it out alive.

The boys continued inching along the hallway until they saw it open into a large room. Cautiously they remained in the poorly lit hallway, listening and watching. Suddenly a moan echoed through the hall, followed by a woman crying, and then silence. Manuel pulled Arlo close.

"Somebody's in that room," whispered Manuel. Arlo nodded his head in agreement.

"Let's move closer. We don't have a choice."

The boys crept closer to the room, pausing whenever they heard a sound. As they moved nearer, a wooden table came into view—a table filled with knives and strangely shaped weapons that neither of the boys had ever seen.

"Holy shit!" whispered Manuel. Arlo put his index finger over his lips to calm his friend and continued tiptoeing forward. Finally, they arrived at the entrance. Slowly the boys peeked around the corner.

The ceiling and the walls had mud smeared all over them, and the floor was covered in about two inches of excrement. Half-submerged in the sludge were a dozen small, barred cages filled with people.

One of the men in the cages saw the boys watching them from the hallway.

"Oh, thank God! You gotta get me out of here," he cried, extending his hand through the bars. Arlo didn't move. Instead, he continued watching the man, afraid of who had put him there; he could see human bones in the bottom of the cage.

"Come on! Get me out of here!" the man screamed, yanking on the cage in frustration. Arlo was about to walk out when Manuel grabbed his arm.

"Dude! You're not really going out there, are you?"

"We gotta get those people out. They could easily be us."

"Aren't you afraid of who put them there?"

"Who, John?"

Arlo jerked free and walked into the room with a reluctant Manuel in tow. As soon as they entered, the prisoners burst into a cry.

"Get me out!"

"Please! I have a son!"

"Come on, boys! Get me the fuck out of here!"

"I'll pay you, boys! I've got a lot of money!"

Manuel shook his head in disbelief.

"Hey, Arlo. All these people are adults. Where are the kids?"

Arlo's eyes fell on a naked woman lying in her muddy cell, crying. He knelt before the woman and jerked on her cage but couldn't open it. The woman raised herself from the sludge and locked her eyes on Arlo.

"It's okay if you can't get me out. Let me die here. I can feel those things growing inside me; you shouldn't get too close. It's just . . ."

The woman's voice trailed away, and she began sobbing.

"Who's going to take care of my Trevor? Please! Don't let them turn me into one of those zombie things. Trevor couldn't take that. Let me die!"

The woman's words touched Manuel, and he walked over and jerked on the woman's cage but couldn't open it.

"How did you guys get in here?" asked Manuel, continuing to struggle to free the woman.

Arlo noticed a man sitting silently in his cage, watching them. The man's calm demeanor frightened him. Arlo began jerking on the closest cell, trying to free the man inside while staring at the emotionless man, watching him was like witnessing a person stripped of all hope.

Finally, the emotionless man spoke, his voice a deep, scratchy hum of exhaustion.

"It's over for us. If you boys are smart, you will get out of here before it comes back."

"It?" asked Arlo and Manuel in unison.

Suddenly the cage on the other side of the room began rattling and got the boys' attention. There was a man inside that was so thin, his hipbones were showing. He was foaming at the mouth, and mud was pouring from his eyes.

"Get it out of me. Get it out. . . ."

Suddenly the man thrust himself against the bars close to Arlo and spoke directly to him.

"I can see it's inside you, too, and it wants to eat."

The man moaned and fell against the back of the cage.

Suddenly an enormous translucent worm with silver teeth burst from his chest and began snapping at the air. The creature didn't eat the man. Instead, it tried to go back into the gaping hole in his chest.

"Holy shit!" yelled Manuel.

But Arlo was worried about something else. He grabbed Manuel by the arm and pulled him away from the cage.

"Quick! We need to hide! John's coming!"

Arlo remembered the table filled with weapons and ran there with Manuel. Just as they ducked underneath the table, they heard heavy footsteps approaching from a separate hallway on the other side of the room. Manuel grabbed a long knife from the table and motioned for Arlo to do the same. Just as Arlo grabbed a knife, footsteps arrived in the room. Once again, the caged prisoners started pleading for their lives.

"Please! Let me out! I'll do anything you want!"

"We have families! Let us go!"

"What do you want from me?"

Arlo looked out from his hiding space and began to tremble in fear —it was the hooded figure he'd seen at the museum.

"John," Arlo mouthed; he was too afraid to say the man's name for fear of the monster discovering they were in the room. But he knew it was him; the creature's presence was undeniable within the stench of that place—that prison of torture.

Arlo watched him move, an evil glide of sorts, a deliberate momentum meant to suck all the oxygen out of the room and replace it with fear and pain; John was an instrument of hell, come to take what belonged to him.

Arlo had to tell himself not to look at John's face; he'd seen it before, and it terrified him. Arlo was happy there was a hiding space with such limited visuals; he didn't need a reminder of the three terrible faces sitting atop John's monstrous shoulders.

Still, Arlo couldn't help watching the monster as he moved through the room. John's hands were enormous, stretching out from underneath the robe like gigantic crabs. He towered over everything like a transmitter of evil, enjoying seeing his victims trembling in the cages.

Although thick mud was all over the room, John's thunderous steps shook the ground beneath them. The footsteps passed the others and stopped in front of the injured man with the worm in his chest. The creature raised itself out of the man's bloody chest and stared at John with cat-like eyes. It turned and attacked the man, biting chunks of meat out of the man's face before turning to face John once more. John extended one of his long hands above the cage, and the worm jumped into it, wrapped its body around John's wrist, and emitted a metallic scream so loud that Arlo and Manuel had to cover their ears.

"What is he doing?" whispered Arlo.

John raised his hand to his face and suddenly began shaking.

"Is he . . . Is he eating it?" asked Manuel.

John's body trembled faster as the worm's screams grew louder. Finally, the worm's cries stopped, and John dangled the limp creature in his hand above the cage. A dark shiny substance poured out of the worm's mouth and spread like a blanket onto the corpse.

"Oh my God," whispered Arlo, suddenly grabbing his chest.

As if hearing Arlo's words, the prisoners all began complaining of discomfort.

"I think I'm going to be sick."

"Someone, please help me!"

"What's happening to me? I'm dying."

The boys watched in astonishment as the other prisoners fell limp in their cells, foaming at the mouth with helpless eyes trained on their master.

"Arlo . . ." whispered Manuel, laying down his weapon and grabbing his chest. "Something's h-happening. I don't feel so good."

Arlo felt horrible, too. He laid down his weapon and turned to respond to Manuel when suddenly he felt a rush of pressure in his chest. Seconds later, they both laid helpless against the wall with white foam pouring from their mouths.

Although they were incapacitated, Arlo kept his eyes on John. The monster continued holding the worm over the corpse until the tar-like substance blanketed the body. Suddenly the body jerked, and then all the flesh melted away, leaving only bones. John lowered himself to his knees and placed his face next to the cage; A loud suction noise sounded, and he began shaking. The black tar moved across the floor and disappeared into John's hooded robe.

John stood, stepped back from the cage, and walked to the next prisoner, causing the terrified man inside to recoil in fear against the back of the enclosure.

"Please . . . Not me."

John reached inside the cage and touched the man's leg, paralyzing him and making him drool.

As soon as the monster moved away from the cage, the pain in Arlo's chest subsided, and he could move again. He quickly turned to Manuel and shook him.

"Mani, you okay?"

"Yeah. What the hell happened to us?"

"Remember your dreams? We have worms in us."

"Shit! I knew it!"

"Did you see what he's doing? Everyone in this room is that thing's food, and he will eat all of us unless we do something about it."

"What do you want to do?"

Arlo grabbed his knife from the floor.

"We only have one chance. While his back is to us, we can try to kill him."

"You sure, Arlo? Look how big he is."

"We don't have a choice. We have to try to kill him while he's not looking because we can't do it straight up."

The boys rose from the floor and prepared to attack. A voice echoed throughout the room just as they were about to run out from their hiding place.

"You have come."

Arlo and Manuel looked at one another.

"I've been waiting for you. Take the final step and give your souls to us."

Arlo grasped the knife firmly and turned to Manuel.

"We have to do it now!"

Arlo stepped out from his hiding place and raised the knife. He was about to sprint toward John but suddenly stopped—a piercing pain shot through his back, causing him to drop the knife.

"What is this? Mani, help me. I think it's the worms," he moaned in agony, turning around to his friend. Arlo's eyes widened in surprise as soon as he saw Manuel— standing before him, holding a bloody knife and shaking his head.

"I'm sorry, Arlo, but you have to die. John told me it's the only way."

Arlo looked at his best friend in disbelief, blood pouring from the hole in his back.

"But . . . you're supposed to be my friend. How could you do this to me?"

With a smile on his face, Manuel moved closer to Arlo.

"We'll always be best friends. I'm sorry, Arlo."

Manuel grabbed Arlo's hair and jerked his head back. With one movement, he ran the blade across his friend's neck, causing Arlo's warm red blood to shoot into his face like a sprinkler. Arlo's eyes met Manuel's once more, and Arlo cried inside; Manuel's betrayal cut worse than the knife, a friendship proven meaningless through John's tampering.

Arlo felt his soul moving beyond his body and looked up into nothingness. He never felt his body crash to the dirty floor, nor the tearing of his chest cavity as the worm burst from his chest and ripped off chunks of his face. He laid gurgling for a moment, but he wasn't there. It was only his body's natural response to fighting the inevitable.

It Was You All Along

Manuel stared emotionless at Arlo's corpse lying in filth on the floor. He remembered all the conversations the two friends shared: their dreams about jobs, which girls they liked, and the universities they hoped to attend. But Manuel also remembered the conversations they didn't have: the talks he'd instead had with a dark figure in his dreams, conversations that touched parts of his soul unlike anything could. In time, those discussions moved from Manuel's dreams to reality; a tall, dark figure cloaked in a filthy leather black robe began visiting Manuel nightly to discuss death, destruction, power, and betrayal. Within those conversations, Manuel always felt a sense of regret about what would come to pass, but he knew there was no other way. Arlo had to die because John told Manuel it needed to happen. His death would be Manuel's transition to power.

Manuel looked at the people in the cages, all silent, shivering at the possibility that their deaths would come next. But Manuel didn't feel anything for them. He'd decided long ago that this was what he wanted. Even before he began picking pieces of his father's corpse out of his teeth, Manuel knew he wanted this—to be whole in a world of the weak as someone unbreakable and powerful, towering over the weaklings.

Soon his eyes fell on the figure lurking next to the cage. Manuel stepped over Arlo's body and walked over to the monster.

"I've done everything you've asked, John," said Manuel. "Now give it to me."

The towering figure moved closer and let his robe fall to the ground.

"Oh my God!" exclaimed Manuel.

John's three faces were a twisted mess of slime, mud, and blood, all juxtaposing horror on one skull. The three faces saw the fear on Manuel's face and burst into laughter.

"You need not cry out for a thing that does not exist!"

"You are a God!

"Together, we will cover this world in the misery of Balam."

Manuel's eyes dropped to the monster's chest—he could see his father's face stretching John's skin, trying to break free.

"Mani! Please help me! I need you!"

But Manuel didn't cry. Instead, his face turned cold, and he rose to his feet.

"Give it to me now!"

John extended his hand to the door, and Manuel turned to look— it was the old woman from the pit with mud pouring out of her eyes. The sightless old woman stopped at the table filled with weapons and ran her fingers across the knives. The old witch smiled when her hand fell on the blade she wanted—an enormous knife shaped like a hook. She grabbed the cutting tool and inched through the room to Manuel. Finally standing before the boy, she smiled as thick mud poured steadily from her eyes.

"I can see you!" she whispered.

Manuel closed his eyes and tried emptying his mind. The witch smiled at Manuel's behavior and turned to speak to John.

"You've prepared him well. His mind is ready to receive Balam's gift."

The old woman placed her hand on John's deformed chest and pushed, causing Manuel's father to cry in agony.

"Please, Manuel! I'm your father! It hurts so much!"

There was a crunching sound beneath the witch's hand, and Manuel's father went silent. The woman took the knife and plunged it into John's chest, causing the monster to throw back his enormous head and release a demonic yell throughout the room.

"AAAAHHHH!"

Manuel watched, horrified, as the gaping wound on the creature's chest grew larger, displaying John's pounding heart and organs inside his ribcage. There was movement, and Manuel saw something inside John's ribs—something with red skin and black eyes, like a snake or perhaps a long lizard, moving inside him.

"What's that?" asked Manuel automatically. With a smile, the old woman acknowledged the boy's question and thrust her hands inside the wound. John's three faces went unconscious as the woman sloshed around inside the enormous man, digging, searching for something.

"Don't worry. I have them," the old woman whispered.

Suddenly she stopped searching and began pulling.

"Sheeee-la," she chanted, spraying mud everywhere as she struggled. "Sheeee-la."

Soon the witch's hands reappeared, covered in large blisters. Twisting in her hands were two thick worms glowing like fire. The monsters shrieked in her grasp, snapping their enormous mouths at the woman's face, but she had them firmly in her grip.

"Moos-ti-Kah-nita! Moos-ti-Kah-nita!" she chanted.

Suddenly the snakes turned to red stone and extended from the wound in John's chest. Satisfied, the witch turned to Manuel.

"Rise, my master," she instructed.

Unable to hide his nervousness, Manuel rose to his feet and moved closer to John. The stench from the creature's body smelled like roadkill rotting in the hot sun. The woman touched Manuel on his head, and Manuel jumped because of the iciness of her grasp.

"What . . . What are you doing?"

"Relax. The transition will be over soon."

But Manuel's body soon grew hot like fire, and he screamed.

"PLEASE! IT BURNS!"

"Calm yourself, my king. Allow Balam to take control of your spirit."

Manuel's eyes started bleeding, and a strong wind blew through the room. Manuel lowered his head and began growling like a creature from hell, biting at the air and speaking in a strange, demonic voice.

"Give him to me, you bitch! Let me eat his soul!"

The witch tried to calm Manuel, but he bit off her fingers as soon as she reached out for him.

"I SAID GIVE HIM TO ME! NOW!"

The woman was unaffected by the demon's outburst and calmly moved behind Manuel. With blood gushing from her wounded hand, she thrust Manuel into John's chest with all her might and held him there. Suddenly the snakes came back to life and shot into Manuel's chest, spraying his blood all over the floor.

"Di-Kah-Liiiiiii," the woman screamed. Black sludge shot out of the woman's eyes with such force that it sent her flying across the room. The mud sprayed out randomly and then gathered in a massive ball of liquid before landing on Manuel and John, covering their bodies in a black cocoon.

The other prisoners in the room continued screaming while the old lady sat against the wall, bleeding and watching the shadows moving inside the liquid. Finally, the colossal liquid ball exploded, sending Manuel's unconscious body sliding across the floor.

"My master?" asked the old woman as she climbed to her feet. Finally, coughing and dizzy, Manuel crawled to his knees and vomited, spraying the black liquid in his lungs onto the floor.

"I am here," Manuel whispered.

Manuel stood and walked over to the pool of sludge left by his transformation. The only thing left of John's body was a child's bones, tiny with thousands of bite marks all over them. Crudely, Manuel kicked the deformed skull across the floor.

"It is time for hell's rise. Burn the incubation pit and let the dog feast. Initiation has begun."

The old woman bowed to Manuel.

"Yes, Master."

Slowly, Manuel walked out of the room, and the old woman followed. She paused briefly at the entrance, waved her mutilated hand, and all the cages popped open.

"Thank God!" yelled one man before scrambling out. He paused, unsure of where to go, and went through the hallway on the other side of the room. The other prisoners stared after the man, uncertain of their freedom. After a few seconds, a woman opened her cage and ran out. Then they all sprinted out of the room into a long dark hallway, where they stopped.

"Wait! What's that?"

The dog beast was at the far end of the hallway, eyes glowing and growling, chained to a wall and feasting on a corpse. The monster stopped eating and glared at the people standing at the other end of the hallway.

"Oh my God! Go back! Go back!" yelled the first prisoner.

But there were too many of them. They all fell clumsily over one another, trying to escape. The beast rose from the carcass it was eating and released a terrifying howl. Blood dripping from its face. It jumped on the closest man, ripping his ribcage from his chest with one swipe of its monstrous paw. The next prisoner, the woman that had begged for her child, looked into the creature's eyes and fell to her knees, praying for mercy. But the monster's viciousness was indiscriminate; it bit off her head with its enormous mouth and swallowed it before jumping on the closest man and gnawing his stomach until the man's body split in half.

Finally, when the screams ceased and there was no more fresh blood to paint the walls, the monster went to each victim, taking what it wanted; it ate the intestines of some, the legs of others, and the faces of a few. And when it had eaten its fill of blood and flesh, the creature laid down in the dark hallway and slept.

38

The Gathering

When Manuel walked out of the old house, he saw hundreds of children standing before him. He took in a deep breath and sighed. He could feel the worms growing inside a large portion of the children— but not all of them. The worms were whispering to him:

"We've found you."

"Yes! We've found the one."

Suddenly the sightless witch exited the house and stood on the porch by Manuel's side.

"What do you ask of me, Master?"

"From this moment forth, you shall refer to me as *John*. His soul has bonded with mine in the fires of hell, and we are one spirit."

"Yes, John."

John turned to face the old woman and touched her gently on her face. As soon as he did, a burst of light shot from his fingertips, and a strange red fire spread over the woman's body. In seconds, her mangled hand was whole, and the mud disappeared from her eyes.

"The time of the serpent has passed."

"Yes, John. We used them to try and find you."

"And so you have found my spirit. Your search has concluded. We must rid ourselves of the remaining carriers—they serve no purpose."

"Yes, John."

The witch nodded to a boy, and he took off running. In seconds he was back with the can of gasoline Arlo had brought to the forest. The witch took it from him and passed it to a little girl standing nearby. Without saying a word, the child poured the gasoline on her body. Afterward, she moved through the crowd and gave the can to another child. And then another. And another.

Finally, when the can was empty, the child walked to the front of the group and gave the empty can to the old woman. The woman raised her hand, and the children with gasoline on their bodies suddenly burst into flame. None of them screamed as the fire engulfed their bodies; they all stared motionless at their master until they fell to the ground and burned to ash.

When the flames from the last child stopped burning, John surveyed the field—there were still over one hundred children standing before him.

"Now is the time to build Balam's army. Begin phase one."

The witch walked into the old house and retrieved a knife. Without hesitation, she walked to John and shoved it into his stomach. John didn't react. Instead, he reached into his jeans, pulled out a cell phone, and dialed 911. After a short delay, he spoke.

"Please, help me! This crazy family has me trapped in their house, and they killed my friends. Now they're going to kill me. Please! Send someone quick! I'm in the Black Hills Forest."

John hung up the phone and passed it to the witch. Slowly, he laid himself on the ground.

"Prepare to cover the world in darkness."

The old woman walked back into the house, and the other children dispersed into the forest while John on his back, waiting for the police to arrive.

39

You Belong

A corpse laid in the mud beneath the old house, staring into nothingness. Although death surrounded it, the corpse was the centerpiece of that nightmare—torn apart by the betrayal of a friendship that had nourished him for many years.

Suddenly there was an explosion, and the screams of evil creatures filled the room. If the corpse were alive, it would know who those shrieks belonged to—the thousands of soul-sucking worms in the lake just beyond the corridor—someone had set them ablaze.

In time, smoke billowed into the room, and the screams of the monsters grew faint. The odor of the infested mud grew as strong as pneumonia as it pushed through the caverns.

Still, the body laid motionless. The life inside it was gone, and no matter what happened in the world around it, the corpse was void of life.

But . . .

Suddenly there was a noise—a splashing just beyond the other corridor. The demonic dog let out a long, low growl and then a painful yelp. Next came the splashing of feet in the mud—dragging, sliding, and dragging again. Someone was there. The feet finally arrived at the corpse.

"Arlooooooo," the voice moaned.

But Arlo did not move. He was dead.

Finally, a hand reached into the gaping hole in his chest. There was the slippery thrashing of organs and then . . .

Arlo's eyes opened. He could see again. He wanted to scream, but the rush of pain he felt coursing through his body paralyzed him.

"Come with me," the voice whispered. "I will help you."

Arlo looked up and saw who was standing over him—Isadora, her mangled body, leaking fluids with a huge gaping hole in her torso. Her eyes were white with death, yet she was still moving, displaying a small smile beneath a face of terror. Arlo wanted to say something to her, but his voice was gone.

Isadora knew Arlo was trying to speak, and she shook her head.

"Nooooo," she moaned, black ooze leaking from her mouth. "Save your strength."

Arlo's eyes looked around the room as he struggled to comprehend what had happened. Was he alive or dead? Where was Manuel? Had he evaded death?

Suddenly, Isadora grabbed Arlo's ankle and began pulling him through the darkness.

"Soon," she whispered as she pulled him. "We go to war."

Nathan Jay is a fantasy and horror author living in Washington DC.

9 789898 884772 4